Allie Finkle's RULES -for- GIRLS

Book Two: The New Girl

Books by MEG CABOT

Allie Finkle's Rules for Girls #1: *Moving Day*
Allie Finkle's Rules for Girls #2: *The New Girl*

FOR TEENS

Airhead
All-American Girl
Ready or Not
Teen Idol
How to Be Popular
Pants on Fire
Jinx
Nicola and the Viscount
Victoria and the Rogue

The Princess Diaries series
The Mediator series
I-800-Where-R-You series
Avalon High series

**For a complete list of Meg Cabot's books,
please visit www.megcabot.com**

MEG CABOT

Allie Finkle's RULES for GIRLS

Book Two: The New Girl

SCHOLASTIC PRESS · NEW YORK

An Imprint of Scholastic Inc.

Library of Congress Cataloging-in-Publication Data

Cabot, Meg.

The new girl / by Meg Cabot. — 1st ed.

p. cm. — (Allie Finkle's rules for girls ; bk. 2)

Summary: Guided by her rules, nine-year-old Allie works to get
past being just the new girl at school, eagerly awaits the arrival of
her kitten, and faces turmoil when her grandmother visits while
the family is still settling into their new home.

ISBN-13: 978-0-545-04049-5

ISBN-10: 0-545-04049-3

[1. Schools — Fiction.   2. Bullies — Fiction.   3. Grandmothers — Fiction.
4. Rules (Philosophy) — Fiction.   5. Moving, Household — Fiction.   6. Best
friends — Fiction.   7. Friendship — Fiction.   8. Family life — Fiction.]

I. Title.

PZ7.C11165New 2008

[Fic] — dc22

2007050719

10   9   8   7   6   5   4   3   2

Printed in the U.S.A.

First edition, September 2008

The display type was set in Chaloops and Yellabelly.
The text type was set in Centaur MT Regular.
Book design by Elizabeth B. Parisi

For everyone who has
ever been bullied

Many thanks to Beth Ader, Rachel Breinen, Jennifer Brown, Barbara Cabot, Michele Jaffe, Laura Langlie, Abigail McAden, and especially Benjamin Egnatz

Allie Finkle's RULES for GIRLS

Book Two: The New Girl

RULE #1

When You Are Starting Your First Day Ever at a Brand-new School, You Have to Wear Something Good, So People Will Think You're Nice

Mom didn't think I should wear a skirt with jeans on my first day at my new school.

"Allie," she kept saying. "You can wear a skirt *or* jeans. But not both at the same time."

This argument was not helping the nervous butterflies that were fluttering around in my stomach, considering the fact I was less than one hour away from starting my first day at Pine Heights Elementary, my brand-new school.

I tried to explain about how my new plaid skirt flared out when I twirled around. Which was totally great, and a very important trick to be able to do, especially on your first day at a new school.

Except what was going to happen if I climbed the jungle gym and hung upside down at recess?

I'm not saying I was *going* to do this. I'm just saying it *could* happen, and if it did, and all I was wearing was a skirt, the boys on the playground would totally see my underwear.

This was not something you would particularly want to happen on the first day at a brand-new school.

I don't see how Mom couldn't tell that this was a problem.

Fortunately, it was a problem that was easily solved. It was solved by wearing jeans under my skirt.

"Allie," Mom said. "Why don't you wear tights under your skirt? Or leggings?"

Which was a nice idea. But, as I reminded her, all my tights and leggings were still packed — along with all of my pajamas — since we had just moved to our new house two days before. And we couldn't find the box they were packed in. We could only find the box with my jeans, shirts, and skirts in it.

My tights, leggings, and pajamas were not the only things we'd packed and couldn't find. We also couldn't find the hair dryer, the cereal bowls, and most of the pots and pans.

But this was okay, because our new stove hadn't come yet, so we had nothing to cook on, anyway.

Personally, I didn't see why wearing my plaid skirt with jeans was such a bad thing. I thought my skirt looked really, really good with jeans. So good that I decided to wear it on my first official day at Pine Heights Elementary.

Because *When you are starting your first day ever at a brand-new school, you have to wear something good, so people will think you're nice.* This is a rule.

First impressions are important. Everyone knows this.

It's true that I had already been to Pine Heights Elementary School once before and met my new teacher (Mrs. Hunter) and some of my new classmates (Caroline and Sophie, and of course Erica).

But while I'd already been over to Erica's house multiple times, and she'd been over to mine, because we lived next door to each other, I hadn't really gotten to know Caroline and Sophie yet (other than playing a game they'd made up called queens with them at recess the day I'd met them).

And there were still lots of people I hadn't met at all yet, and I wanted to make sure I got off on the right foot with them.

Getting off on the right foot with people is important. If you don't get off on the right foot with people, it could ruin your whole year.

Which was why I knew wearing a skirt with jeans would be just the right thing to do.

It was just too bad Mom didn't think so.

Fortunately, Mom had bigger things to worry about. Like that my little brother Kevin wanted to wear his pirate costume to his first day of kindergarten at Pine Heights Elementary. Really, in comparison, my wearing a skirt with jeans was nothing.

"But Halloween was last month, Kevin," Mom kept saying.

"I don't care," Kevin said. "It's important to make a good first impression. Allie said so. Allie said it was a rule."

Mom was too busy chasing Kevin around, trying to get him out of his pirate costume, to notice I was still wearing my skirt with my jeans. So I sneaked into the kitchen to see what was for breakfast. What was for breakfast was popcorn.

"I can't find the cereal bowls," Dad explained.

"We could just eat it out of the box," my brother Mark said, stuffing popcorn into his mouth. Mark is in the second grade. Mark did not have butterflies in his stomach about his first day at a brand-new school. Mark never has butterflies about anything, such as, for instance, jumping off the roof of his friend Sean's house, which he did once, thus breaking his arm. This is because Mark doesn't think about anything except bugs. And sports. And possibly trucks.

"Once at Sean's house," Mark said, "we poured milk right into the cereal box and ate out of it with spoons."

"That's disgusting," I said.

"No, it wasn't," Mark said.

"I'm sure the milk leaked," I said. "Out of the box and all over the place."

"No, it didn't," Mark said. "Because of the seal-tight plastic bag inside."

"Well, I'm not doing that," I said. "I'm not sharing a box of cereal with you. I don't want your germs."

"We have the same germs," Mark said. "Because we're related."

"Actually, we don't," I said. "Because I don't pick my nose and eat it like some people I could mention."

"The thing is," Dad said while Mark was denying that he picks his nose and eats it, "no one is sharing a box of cereal. Because I can't find the spoons, either."

"What's going on in here?" Mom said, running into the kitchen. She was holding Kevin's pirate hat, but she didn't have the rest of Kevin. That's because he'd disappeared into one of the many secret passageways of our new house, which is more than a hundred years old. "Why does it smell like popcorn?"

"That's what we're having for breakfast," Mark said.

"No," Mom said. "How did this happen? Whose idea was this?"

Mark and I both pointed at Dad. He said, "I don't see what the problem is. Popcorn is made of corn. People eat cornflakes for breakfast all the time."

"Popcorn has no nutritional value," Mom said.

"Yes, it does," I said. "Popcorn is high in fiber. Fiber is good for you." I know this because I did a report on fiber for science once. Corn, which is something they grow a lot of in my home state, is full of fiber. *You need a lot of fiber in your diet to help digest your food.* This is a rule.

"But they haven't had any dairy," Mom protested.

"I put butter on it," Dad said. "And they've got orange juice."

Mark and I raised our measuring cups of orange juice to show her. We were drinking out of measuring cups because Dad couldn't find the drinking cups.

Mom looked at the ceiling. "Please don't tell your new teachers you had popcorn for breakfast today," she said before racing out of the kitchen after Kevin, who was hiding until the last possible minute so Mom would have no choice but to let him wear his pirate costume to school.

I knew the feeling.

"My new teacher, Mr. Manx, would think it was cool if I told him I had popcorn for breakfast," Mark said. "Probably."

"Well," Dad said, "Mom would appreciate it if you didn't tell him, anyway. When you come home for lunch, things will be more organized. I promise."

That was when the doorbell rang. The doorbell on our new house isn't a normal doorbell where you push a button and it goes *ding-dong*. That's because our house is so old, the doorbell is a crank that you turn, and it rings a bell attached to the other side of the wall that goes *brrrring*, like a bicycle bell.

But if you cup your hand over the bell part while someone is turning the crank, it just goes *brrurp*. We found this out after playing around with the doorbell so many times that Mom finally said, *No child whose last name is Finkle may touch the doorbell or they will not be allowed to watch television for two weeks.* This is a rule. Not one of mine, one of the family rules.

"That's Erica!" I yelled because I was so excited. Erica had said she'd stop by to walk to school with me on my first day.

I raced to the front door and flung it open. Erica was standing there in her hat and coat, looking as excited as I was.

"Hi, Allie!" she yelled.

"Hi, Erica!" I yelled back.

"I can't believe it's your first day at Pine Heights!" Erica yelled.

"I can't believe it, either!" I yelled back.

Then we both jumped up and down for a while until Mark came and said, "Girls," disgustedly, then brushed past us and ran outside to join some boys he saw riding by on their bikes.

"Wait!" Mom screamed from deep inside the house.

"Why does your house smell like popcorn?" Erica wanted to know.

"Because we had it for breakfast," I said, getting my hat

and coat. "We packed the cereal bowls and can't find them. I can't find my tights or leggings, either. That's why I'm wearing jeans with this skirt." I twirled to show Erica my skirt.

"Wow, that skirt is so cute," she said. "It's like my sister's skirt for baton twirling."

This made me really happy to hear, because Erica's older sister, Melissa, who goes to the middle school and is an expert baton twirler, is really, really cool, even though she mostly doesn't speak to us and stomps away with her nose in the air whenever we're around.

"Here we are," Mom said, showing up with Kevin just as Erica and I were about to walk out the door.

Erica and I looked at Kevin. He was still wearing black pants, black boots, and a white shirt with long puffy sleeves. Mom had gotten him to give up his red sash, skull and crossbones hat, eye patch, and sword.

"At least she could have let me keep my eye patch," Kevin said, looking sad.

"You look really good," Erica assured him.

"Why don't you just put on normal clothes?" I asked him. It's a pain having such a weird brother. Between him and Mark, I sometimes wonder how I got so cursed in the big sister department.

"*You're* wearing jeans with a skirt," Kevin pointed out.

"I don't want boys to see my underwear in case I hang upside down from the jungle gym," I explained.

"Well, I want everyone to know I'm a pirate," Kevin said.

"They will," Erica assured him.

"Okay," Mom said in a very fake cheerful voice as she appeared with her coat and purse. "Are we ready to walk to school together?"

I could see now that Mark had been smart to run ahead with those boys. *There is nothing wrong with walking to school with your mom and dad on your first day. Except everything.* Which is a rule, by the way.

Or it will be when I write it in my special notebook that I keep in my room for writing rules in.

"We can walk by ourselves," I said quickly.

"What about Kevin?" Mom asked.

"Oh, we'll be happy to walk Kevin, Mrs. Finkle," Erica said, taking Kevin's hand.

I didn't know about that. I mean, no one asked me. I wasn't happy to walk Kevin to school.

But it was better than having my *parents* walk to school with us.

"Sure," I said, taking Kevin's other hand. "We'll walk Kevin."

"Okay," Dad said. He had on his own coat. "You girls walk Kevin. And we'll walk behind you and pretend we don't know you. How's that?"

This wasn't exactly what I had in mind. But it was better than nothing.

"Okay," I muttered.

Erica and I steered Kevin through the door. Outside, the leaves, which had already started changing colors, were beginning to fall from the trees and blanket the sidewalk. It was also cold.

"How come you don't want to walk to school with your parents?" Erica wanted to know. "I think they're funny."

"They're not so funny," I assured her, "once you get to know them."

"Having popcorn for breakfast is funny," Erica said. "My dad would never do that. And letting your brother wear a pirate costume to his first day of school is funny. Even wearing a skirt with jeans is kind of funny — even though it looks really good."

I thought about what Erica said. I didn't think it was true. The Finkles weren't funny. The truth was, Finkles were actually exceptionally talented. Especially my uncle Jay, whom Erica hadn't even met yet because he lived in his own apartment on campus. He was probably the most talented Finkle of all. He could bend one of his toes so far back, it touched the top of his foot. Plus, he had double-jointed thumbs.

I wished I had special skills like that. If I did, I wouldn't have any trouble at all making friends at my brand-new school, or have to wear a special skirt that twirled in order to get people to like me. *If you have special skills or talents, such as having double-jointed thumbs, other people will automatically like you right away* (that's a rule).

It's true that Erica liked me. But she hadn't asked me to be best friends, or anything. Probably a skirt that twirled wasn't going to influence her decision one way or another. But I had to do what I could.

When we were halfway to the school and had reached the stop sign at the first (completely non-busy) street we had to cross to get to Pine Heights, I noticed there were two girls walking toward us from the other direction. Erica said, "Oh, look! It's Caroline and Sophie."

And it was.

"Oh, my gosh, it's your first day," Sophie yelled, jumping up and down when she saw me. "This is so exciting!"

"I know," I yelled back. Because *When someone is yelling at you with excitement, it's polite to yell back.* This is a rule. "I'm so nervous! I have butterflies!"

"Don't be nervous," Caroline said. She was the first one to stop jumping. I was starting to realize this because Caroline is actually quite serious. "Just be yourself. Is this your little brother? Why is he dressed that way?"

"Because I'm a pirate," Kevin informed her.

Caroline looked from Kevin to me.

"He's in kindergarten," I explained with a shrug.

"Are those your *parents*?" Sophie whispered, noticing my parents hanging around behind us. They waved, and Sophie and Caroline waved politely back.

"Just ignore them," I said, pulling on Kevin to get us moving along again.

"They wanted to walk Allie and Kevin to school today," Erica explained. "But Allie wouldn't let them, so now they're just following us."

"Aw," Sophie said. "That's so cute!"

"Allie's dad made them popcorn for breakfast," Erica said. I could tell she was enjoying herself, talking about how funny the Finkles were. This was turning out to be one of her favorite subjects. "Because he couldn't find any cereal bowls!"

"You're not supposed to tell anyone about the popcorn," I reminded her. "Or, at least, not any teachers."

"That's okay," Caroline said. "One time we ran out of sandwich meat, so my dad just made us mustard sandwiches. They weren't very good. My parents are divorced," she explained. "And my big sister and I live with my dad. It can be hard sometimes."

"It must be," I said sympathetically.

"My dad's a really good cook," Sophie said. "Last night for dinner he made us spaghetti Bolognese. My dad does all the cooking in our family, because my mom is working on her dissertation. And besides, she's a terrible cook. She burned potpourri once."

"You can't burn potpourri," Caroline said.

"Yes, you can," Sophie said. "If you go to the mall and leave it simmering on the stove, the water in it evaporates, and then the potpourri smolders, and then the smoke detector goes off, and the neighbors call the fire department. It was so embarrassing."

I appreciated what Caroline and Sophie were trying to do — make the butterflies in my stomach go away.

And it was kind of working. Almost all the butterflies in my stomach had disappeared.

Before I knew it, even though we hadn't been walking particularly fast, our feet were tromping on the dead leaves that lined Pine Heights Elementary's playground. I could hear the shrieks of encouragement as kids (including my brother Mark) played kick ball while waiting for the first bell to ring. I could see people on the swings pumping their legs to go higher and higher. I saw clusters of other kids just standing around, doing nothing but looking at other kids looking at them (which included me).

That's when the butterflies in my stomach came right back. In fact, they turned from butterflies into great big swooping bats banging around inside me. Because I couldn't help thinking, what if none of those kids on the playground liked me? What if the only people who talked to me all day were Erica, Caroline, and Sophie? Which would be okay . . . but I didn't want them to get sick of me, not on my first day. Then I'd have a whole year of no one liking me but those three. That would be terrible! I mean, for them.

It was right then that something truly awful happened.

Kevin let go of my hand and also Erica's and ran toward the jungle gym, I guess because he saw some kids his own age playing on it.

To me Kevin just looked normal. I mean, the fact is, he wears his pirate costume all the time, such as to the grocery store, to story hour at the library, and to Dairy Queen for his favorite cone, vanilla twist butterscotch dip, which he is always careful not to spill on his red sash.

But I heard some of the kids standing in a cluster nearby — they were girls, big girls, too, maybe fifth-grade girls — start to laugh. When I looked over at them, I saw that they were laughing . . . at Kevin! That had to be what they were laughing at, because they were looking right at him.

They were laughing at my brother.

And then they looked over at me. Then they started whispering to one another. Which meant they could only be whispering about me. But why? What was *I* doing wrong? *I* wasn't wearing pirate pants and boots beneath my down parka.

Then I remembered: I was wearing a skirt with jeans. I'd insisted on wearing a skirt with jeans, in spite of the fact that my mom had tried to talk me out of it.

Oh, this was terrible!

And that's when it hit me. Maybe what Erica had said was really true — the Finkles *were* funny. Maybe the Finkles were *too* funny . . . too funny to fit into someplace new. Like a new school . . . a new neighborhood . . . a new anywhere.

Oh, why had I let my parents talk me into moving? Why had I let them convince me to start at a new school, where I didn't really know anyone and where people might think Finkles were funny?

And why — why, oh, why — had I worn a skirt with jeans on my very first day at my brand-new school?

RULE #2

If a Bunch of Fifth-Grade Girls Thinks Your Little Brother Is Cute, Just Go Along with It

Before I could turn around and run all the way home — which was the first thing I thought of doing when I saw them pointing at me and whispering — the big fifth-grade girls started coming toward us.

"Uh-oh," Sophie whispered.

"Uh-oh, is right," I whispered back. "Run!"

But it was too late to run, since the fifth-grade girls were already coming toward us. They were so close, I could practically smell the bubble gum they were chewing.

"We're going to die now," I said faintly, clutching Erica's arm. "Good-bye. It was nice knowing all of you."

"Th-they can't kill us," Sophie stammered. "Mrs. Jenkins, the principal, outlawed killing people on the playground last year."

While this was good to know, I didn't have a whole lot of confidence that these girls were the kind who actually obeyed rules, even those made by the principal. I held on to Erica's arm, feeling a little sad about the fact that I was going to die so soon. I felt like I had so many things left in life that I wanted to do. I had never kissed a boy yet. Not that I really wanted to, but Uncle Jay's girlfriend, Harmony, said kissing was a lot of fun.

And I had also never had one of those blizzard things at Dairy Queen. The ones with the bits of Heath Bar looked good. It was sad I was going to die before ever tasting one.

"I'm sure we'll be able to work something out," Erica said faintly. "They look really nice."

"They don't look so nice to me," Caroline said as the girls loomed over us.

"Hey," one of the fifth-graders said to me. "Are you the New Girl?"

It felt strange to be called the New Girl. At my old school, I hadn't been the New Girl. I'd just been Allie Finkle (except for a few bad days I'd prefer to forget when I'd been Allie Stinkle). And I'd liked it that way just fine.

"Um," I said, my heart beating all hard inside my chest. "Yes?"

"Is that your little brother?" the fifth-grade girl wanted to know.

She pointed at Kevin, who was now hanging upside down on the jungle gym (under the supervision of a teacher, and my parents, who were laughing at him). Kevin, as usual, was enjoying the attention. Kevin didn't have to worry about showing his underwear, of course, since he was wearing his pirate pants and not a skirt.

"Um," I said. I don't know what it was about fifth-graders that made me say "um" a lot. Maybe it was how scary tall they were.

I thought about denying that I was related to Kevin. But

I realized that they would probably just figure it out later, like at some school fair when they saw my whole family doing a cakewalk together or something.

So I said, "Yes."

The biggest fifth-grade girl of all sucked in her breath, and I closed my eyes and waited because I was expecting her to say something like, "Why is he so weird?" or "Why don't you and your family go back to where you came from?"

But instead she cried, "He's so *cute!*"

And then all the other fifth-grade girls squealed, "Oh, my gosh, he is!" and "You're so lucky!" and "What's his name?" and "How can you stand it?" and "Is that a *pirate* costume he's wearing?"

I am not even making this up. That is exactly what they said. Those fifth-grade girls thought my brother in his pirate boots was the cutest thing since cute had been invented or something.

And the next thing I knew, they had rushed over to Kevin and were petting him on the head like he was our dog, Marvin.

And Kevin was loving every minute of it.

"Yes," I overheard him saying. "I guess I *am* pretty cute."

I let go of Erica's arm and the four of us just stood there looking at each other.

"That," Sophie said, "was so close! I really thought those girls were going to kill us."

"They wouldn't have," Erica said. "Really."

"Erica always sees the best in people," Caroline explained to me. "When she isn't keeping the peace. Or trying to, anyway."

"That's not true," Erica protested. Then, when Caroline and Sophie started laughing, she joined them a little sheepishly and said, "Well, maybe it is."

I realized I'd just learned a really valuable rule: *If a bunch of fifth-grade girls thinks your little brother is cute, just go along with it.* It's way better than dying.

It was right then that the bell rang.

"Come on!" Erica said.

We went running over to stand in the line for Mrs. Hunter's fourth-grade class. I smiled when I saw

Mrs. Hunter standing there in the front of the line. She looked so pretty in her sand-colored belted coat, even though her hair wasn't at all long, like my teacher's hair at my old school.

Still, Mrs. Hunter's hair was styled very nicely, and I saw that she had on very nice brown suede boots with high heels.

Mrs. Hunter smiled back when she saw me and gave a little wink.

When other kids saw the wink Mrs. Hunter gave me, they all looked down the line, like, *Who'd she wink at?* Then, when they saw me, they twisted up their faces, and I could hear them whispering, "Who's that?" even though Mrs. Jenkins, the principal, had totally introduced me to the class a few weeks before.

I blushed, knowing they were all thinking, *That must be the New Girl.* Some of the butterflies, which had settled down a little after it became clear the fifth-grade girls weren't going to kill us after all, came fluttering back into my stomach.

Then Mrs. Hunter was saying, "All right, fourth-grade

class, follow me, and keep your line straight and *quiet*, please!" and we were following Mrs. Hunter upstairs to her classroom, which was decorated on the walls with puffy clouds that said things like EVERY CLOUD HAS A SILVER LINING, and silver stars that said things like REACH FOR THE STARS!

Erica showed me where I could hang up my coat and backpack in the cloakroom, but when I got out my pencil case and school supplies I didn't know where to take them. I stood there watching everyone else hurrying to their old-fashioned desks and wondering where I was going to sit until I felt a hand on my shoulder, and then I looked up and saw Mrs. Hunter smiling down at me.

"Welcome, Allie," she said. "We're so glad to have you here. I did a little rearranging last night and made room for a desk for you over by Erica Harrington. I hope that's all right by you —"

I could hear Erica's excited gasp all the way across the room. I glanced in her direction and saw her waving over by the giant windows that looked out across the playground.

"But you two have to promise not to make me regret my decision to let you sit together," Mrs. Hunter went on, very seriously, "by socializing when you're supposed to be paying attention, or I'll have no choice but to split you up. Do you understand?"

I nodded. I couldn't believe my good fortune. This was the best first day of school ever! Aside from the whole parents-following-me-to-school-and-brother-dressed-as-a-pirate thing.

"I understand, Mrs. Hunter," I said.

"Good," she said. "Now go and take your seat."

I hurried to slip behind the desk that had been put at the end of the row beside Erica's, closest to the window. I could feel the gazes of everyone in the classroom as I moved to sit down in it. But that was all right. Even though it was old-fashioned and sort of stuck out a little, like it didn't quite belong, it was my desk, and it was just perfect.

"Good morning, class," Mrs. Hunter said as she walked to the front of the room. "As I'm sure you've noticed by now, we have a new student joining us today. Allie Finkle, would you like to come up to the front of the room and tell us all a little about yourself?"

The truthful answer would have been, no, actually, I would not.

But I could see that I didn't really have much of a choice. *When a grown-up — especially a teacher — asks you to do something, it's really rude not to do it.* That's a rule.

So I stopped arranging my school supplies inside my desk and got up and went to the front of the room where Mrs. Hunter was, and after a nervous glance at her I said, "Well, my name is Allie Finkle, and I just moved here. I live next door to Erica Harrington —"

"That's *me!*" I heard Erica squeal, and a couple of people (well, okay, Sophie and Caroline) laughed.

"Go on," Mrs. Hunter said to me encouragingly. "What are some important things we ought to know about Allie Finkle?"

The first thing that popped into my head, of course,

was what Erica had said earlier — that Finkles were funny.

But I couldn't say that! Because what if Mrs. Hunter asked for examples? I'd have to tell her about how my dad had made popcorn for breakfast, and Mom had specifically told me not to tell any teachers about that.

So I tried to think of something else to say . . . something else important to tell the class that they ought to know about me.

You would think it would be easy to think of something, since I'm me all the time and I know myself so well, and that I would have thought of something right away.

But it's actually really hard to think when you're standing up in front of twenty-five people and all of their gazes are on you.

This made me start feeling really hot. I couldn't stop thinking about how I'd chosen to wear a skirt and jeans. Why had I done this? This is really too many pieces of clothes at one time. Yes, it's excellent for twirling like Erica's sister, Melissa, and for hanging upside down on the jungle gym.

But I couldn't help noticing that only the kinder-gartners at Pine Heights Elementary had been climbing on the jungle gym.

Then, just when I feared I wasn't going to be able to think of anything — anything at all about me that was worth mentioning, except that my uncle Jay had double-jointed thumbs and a turtle named Wang-Ba — I remembered something. Something very important about me!

"I'm getting a kitten," I told Mrs. Hunter's fourth-grade class excitedly. "I'm getting a kitten in a few weeks from the litter of a registered show cat named Lady Serena Archibald who belongs to the mother of a girl at my old school. Lady Serena is a purebred long-haired blue color-point Persian. But her kittens won't be long-haired Persians, because no one knows who the father cat is. But that's okay, because I'll love my kitten no matter what it looks like when it comes out."

"Well," Mrs. Hunter said, smiling, "that's certainly something we didn't know about you before, did we, class? Does anyone have any questions for Allie?"

A very large girl in the back raised her hand. Mrs. Hunter called on her. "Yes, Rosemary?"

"Yeah," Rosemary said. "Was that your little brother who came to school today dressed like a pirate?"

"Yes," I said, thinking she was going to say how cute Kevin was, just like those fifth-grade girls had. Because she was as big as they were. "That was Kevin. He likes pirates. I have another brother, Mark, in the second grade. He likes bugs. Also sports and trucks." I rolled my eyes to show I was not interested in any of these things, and a few people laughed.

But not Rosemary.

"Well," Rosemary said instead, "you might want to tell Kevin that Halloween is over."

Now the class was laughing a lot. At what Rosemary had just said. Mostly just the boys. But still.

"All right," Mrs. Hunter said. Mrs. Hunter hadn't laughed. "That's enough. Does anyone else have any questions for Allie?"

No one else had any questions for me, so Mrs. Hunter thanked me and said that I could go back to my seat.

Which was good, because by then my knees were shaking so hard I could barely stand up anymore. I sank behind my desk, relieved to be sitting down again. I couldn't believe how badly my introducing myself to the class had gone. They'd all laughed! And not with me. *At* me!

"All right, class," Mrs. Hunter said. "Let's get to work, we have a lot to go over this morning. Let's take out our math books and turn right to page fifty-two —"

"You did good!" Erica leaned forward to tell me as she dug around in her desk for her math book.

"I kind of thought so, too," I said. I looked over at Rosemary while my desktop was tilted up and Mrs. Hunter couldn't see us talking. "Is she always like that?"

"Sort of," Erica said. "Don't listen to her! She's mean. That's why Mrs. Hunter has her sit in the back with the boys."

I shook my head. "What do you mean?"

Erica pointed. "See how Mrs. Hunter's desk is back there?"

I looked. Mrs. Hunter's desk, instead of being at the front of the room by the chalkboard, was in the back.

"That way," Erica explained, "during quiet time Mrs. Hunter can keep an eye on the worst-behaved boys who all sit in the back. But when Mrs. Hunter is at the front of the room teaching, Rosemary is back there to keep an eye on things. The boys are afraid of Rosemary because she's so mean, and also much bigger than they are."

"Did Rosemary flunk a grade?" I asked.

"No," Erica said. "Her dad is the football coach at the university. He's six feet seven and weighs almost three hundred pounds."

"Oh," I said. My parents work at the university, too. Only my dad teaches computers, and my mom is an adviser. Neither of them is a sports coach, so they are normal size. "That explains it."

"Allie." Mrs. Hunter's voice floated over from across the top of my desk. I lowered it a little so I could see her. She was looking right at me!

"It's time for math right now," Mrs. Hunter said. "In this class, the time for chitchatting with your neighbor is at recess."

I couldn't believe it! I'd been caught chitchatting with my neighbor, and on my very first day at my brand-new school!

I could feel my face turning bright red, I was so ashamed. I hurried to get out my math book and closed the lid of my desk super softly so as not to draw any more attention to myself. This was so awful! Did Mrs. Hunter hate me? I hoped not. She was so pretty and had been so nice to me. Up until now, anyway.

The thing was, I knew the time for chitchatting with your neighbor was during recess, not math class. I mean, I was a straight-A student back at my old school. I never chitchatted with my neighbor during class time. At least, not very much. I know it sounds babyish, but I wanted to cry, I was so embarrassed for getting in trouble on my very first day.

I tried to turn to the right page of my math book, but I couldn't remember what page Mrs. Hunter had said. I looked over to see what page Erica was on, but I saw she was having the same trouble I was — because she'd been too busy talking to pay attention, too.

Then I noticed that Sophie, in the row of desks in front of mine, was quietly holding her math book up. Why was she holding her math book up like that? Then I realized why! So that I could see what page she was on: 52! Oh, thank you, Sophie Abramowitz! *Thank you!*

I turned to page 52 just as Mrs. Hunter asked, "Who knows the answer to problem number four?" and I saw that problem number four was, *Rashid has forty-nine cents in nineteen coins. How many pennies, nickels, dimes, and quarters is that?*

It took me a moment to figure it out.

"Oh," I cried, raising my hand.

Mrs. Hunter, who'd been about to call on Caroline, who also had her hand raised, looked surprised. Then she said, "Yes, Allie?"

I put my hand down and said, "Two dimes, three nickels, and fourteen pennies."

"That's correct, Allie," Mrs. Hunter said, smiling.

Relief washed over me. I'd gotten it right!

Okay, so my first day had gotten off to a totally terrible start. A mean girl who was much bigger than me thought my little brother was weird, and I'd gotten caught chitchatting with my neighbor by the teacher I'd been hoping to impress.

But at least I'd gotten one answer right!

And some of the fifth-grade girls thought my little brother was cute.

Maybe things would improve. They certainly couldn't get much worse.

That was a rule. Wasn't it?

RULE #3

You Aren't Supposed to Lie to Adults — Unless Lying to Them Will Make Them Feel Better

One of the good things about living so close to where you go to school is that you get to go home for lunch.

So you don't have to worry about whether or not your mom paid your milk money, or if they're serving something gross for the hot lunch that might have tomatoes in it (which you can't eat, because one of your rules is *Never eat anything red*), or who you're going to sit by in the cafeteria, because you won't even be eating lunch in the cafeteria.

Of course, I had to wait outside the kindergarten classroom for Kevin because I promised my mom and dad that I would walk Kevin home, even though Kevin said he wasn't a baby and that he could walk himself home. But that's a lie, because anyone who would wear a pirate costume to school his first day, embarrassing me in front of the entire fourth grade, *is* a baby.

Even if, as he was leaving the classroom, everyone was all, "Oh, good-bye, Kevin, I hope you'll wear your pirate costume tomorrow, too, Kevin, it was so great to meet you, Kevin, you're really special, Kevin," blah-blah. This wasn't the other kindergartners, it was the teacher and the teacher's aides. But it was still pathetic and made me and Erica and Sophie and Caroline (who were waiting with me) want to throw up.

Well, I don't really know if it made them want to throw up, actually, because when Kevin came out of the classroom in his pirate costume, they kind of fought a little over who got to hold his hand on the way home.

"No, you live next door to him," Sophie said to Erica when she offered to hold hands with him. "You get to see him all the time!"

"Yeah," Caroline said. "Let us have a turn. It's only fair."

"Oh, sorry," Erica said, looking horrified. "Of course."

I could see that Caroline was right about Erica. She did *always* seem to try to keep the peace.

I could also see that the whole world was starting to think Kevin was cute. Except me.

"It's okay, girls," Kevin said. "I've got two hands. Caroline and Sophie can each hold one of my hands until the first corner, and then Erica and Allie can each hold one of my hands until we get home."

This kind of made me want to throw up some more. Also kick him. Not hard, but, like, a baby kick, for babies. Especially since I didn't want to hold one of his stinking hands, and neither Sophie nor Caroline nor Erica saw how phony he was being. Kevin may not be the funniest Finkle, but he's definitely the one who thinks he's the cutest right now. And deserves to be kicked the most because of it.

Mark, who'd also been told to wait for Kevin, came around the corner, took one look at my friends fighting over who got to hold Kevin's hands on the way home, rolled his eyes, and took off with his new buddies on one of their dirt bikes.

Mark can be surprisingly smart sometimes, for a second-grader.

Even though I was really hoping we wouldn't, on the way out of school we walked right past the line of kids who were waiting to get their hot lunches. That's because Pine Heights Elementary is very old-fashioned and the cafeteria is also the gym in addition to being the auditorium, and so the kids line up to get their food from this big window in the hallway, which is outside the gym.

So everyone in my whole class (who hadn't brought lunch and was already inside the gym, eating, or had gone home for lunch) saw me, Caroline, Sophie, and Erica walk by with my little brother, Kevin the Cute Pirate.

Everybody was pretty nice about it . . . except Rosemary. She shook her head and said, "I see they *both* wore their Halloween costumes to school today," looking pointedly at my skirt-and-jeans combo, causing all the boys standing in line with her to laugh.

Kevin puffed out his chest and said, "This isn't a costume. I *am* a pirate," getting even more laughs from the crowd, which, Kevin being Kevin, he enjoyed.

But I could feel myself turning even more red than I had in the classroom. I was super relieved when we got outside and I could feel the cool autumn air on my face and hear the leaves crunching beneath my feet.

Even though both Sophie and Caroline assured me, as Erica had, that my skirt looked totally cute with my jeans and not like a costume at all, all the way until we got to the corner where they both had to drop Kevin's hands and make the turn to their own houses, I couldn't get over the feeling that I had chosen the wrong thing to wear to my first day of school — and that, in fact, the whole morning of my first day of school had sort of been a disaster, starting with my breakfast of popcorn and going all the way through to right before lunch (Mrs. Hunter had warned me about the dangers of chitchatting two more times), until now.

Erica seemed to sense how I was feeling, because when we stopped outside my house, she said, "Do you want to come have lunch with me? My mom is making grilled cheese."

"No, thanks," I said, even though grilled cheese is one

of my favorites (so long as it's on white bread and not whole wheat. *Grilled cheese on whole wheat bread is gross.* That's a rule). "I'll meet you outside to walk back to school together after lunch, though."

Erica said okay and went on to her house. I followed Kevin inside and wasn't too cheered up when Mom greeted us in the kitchen with a happy announcement: "I found the cereal bowls! No more popcorn for breakfast!"

"Did you find my leggings?" I wanted to know.

"Not yet," she said, her head popping up from the box she was digging through. "But I made huge amounts of progress here in the kitchen while you kids were gone this morning. I found all the pots and pans. Now all we need is the stove, and we'll be set!"

"What I really need is my leggings," I said.

"I know, honey," Mom said. "I'm sure they're around here somewhere. I'll probably stumble across them this afternoon. In the meantime, I've got your favorite for lunch — Hot Pockets! Now why don't you sit down and eat before they get cold. Mark's already finished half of his. I can't wait to hear how your first day is going so far."

But I could hardly get a word in about my day what with my brothers going on and on about their days. Neither of them had gotten in trouble (three times) for chitchatting with his neighbor. Neither of them had gotten made fun of for wearing a skirt with jeans. Neither of them had a girl like Rosemary in his class.

By the time Kevin finally got done going on and on about how cute everyone thought he was and how fantastic his macaroni-and-glue masterpiece had turned out, and Mark had finished gushing over how his new teacher, Mr. Manx, had let him feed the class newts, and his new friend, Jeff, had given him a ride on the handlebars of his dirt bike (which earned him a lecture from Mom since Mark hadn't been wearing his helmet), I didn't even feel like talking. I just wanted to go upstairs, take off my skirt, and go back to school to start my first day over.

"And how's your day going so far, Allie?" Mom wanted to know.

"Fine," I said.

"That's it?" Mom asked. "Just fine? How do you like Mrs. Hunter? Who do you get to sit by? Is it as hard as your old school, or is it easier? Have you made any new friends?"

"Fine, I told you; I get to sit by Erica; it's the same; I'm friends with Caroline and Sophie. Can I go now?"

Mom stared at me. She had on her oldest clothes because she'd taken time off from her job and had been busy all morning unpacking. Her T-shirt said PEARL JAM, which is an old band that Dad likes.

"You *may* go, after you finish your milk," Mom said. "Allie, are you sure everything is all right? You seem upset about something."

"Well, I'm not," I said. "Except that *some* people should realize Halloween was last month."

Kevin looked at me and smiled. "You know what? I'm going to help Mom look for your leggings while you're at school this afternoon, Allie."

"Oh," Mom said, smiling at him. "Isn't that nice of Kevin, Allie?"

I glared at him. *Little brothers can be such total phonies sometimes.*

That's a rule. No, that's not even a rule. That's a *fact.*

During lunch recess, Erica and I met Caroline and Sophie back on the playground, and we went to the secret spot behind the bushes where, the first day I met them, we'd played a game called queens. That's where all of us pretend to be queens doing battle with an evil war-lord who wants to marry Sophie, only she doesn't want to marry him because he's evil, and also because she gave her heart to another. I asked Sophie who she gave her heart to, and she said she gave it to Peter Jacobs, and when I asked who that was, she showed me through the bushes. He was a fourth-grader in Mrs. Danielson's class who happened to be playing kick ball with my brother. He was taller than all the other fourth-grade boys, and also taller than Rosemary. I noticed that he seemed to be kind to all the younger kids who were play-ing, not calling them names when they missed the ball (unlike Rosemary) and yelling to them encouragingly (also unlike Rosemary).

Also, he was wearing a very pretty blue sweater.

I could see why Sophie gave her heart to him, and I told her I approved.

So I decided to put Peter in our game (only not tell him, of course. It's just pretend). I dubbed him Prince Peter and told Sophie that he was her betrothed (I don't know if it's okay for a prince to marry a queen but it's just pretend, anyway, so who cares?).

We were defending pretend Prince Peter from the evil warlord when the bell rang and we had to go get in line for class. We were laughing because Peter had no idea he was a prince, when Rosemary came up to me and went, "Hey, where'd your skirt go?" only not in a nice way like she was genuinely concerned I might have lost it in a freak skirt accident or something.

Up until that moment none of the other girls had noticed I'd changed out of my skirt when I'd gone home for lunch, or at least they hadn't mentioned it. Trust Rosemary to have pointed it out for them.

"Oh," I said, feeling myself blushing, "I changed because, um, I — I was hot."

I don't know why I said I was hot. It was a stupid thing to say because it was actually pretty cold out.

But it was the only reason I could think of for why I had changed, other than the real reason, which was that I had changed because Rosemary had made fun of me. And I didn't want her to know I'd changed because of *that*. Because *You can't let a bully know she's bothering you, otherwise the bully wins*. That's a rule.

"Yeah," Rosemary said with an unpleasant laugh. "Right!"

"Never mind her," Erica said in a quiet voice.

"Yeah," Sophie said. "She's just plain mean."

I knew Rosemary was mean. But that didn't help me know why she was being so mean to *me*. Or what I was going to do about it.

After lunch, we had music, and after music, we had English. For English, Mrs. Hunter asked us each to write a personal essay about a future goal. She told us to be sure to check our spelling, because next week we'd be having our big spelling bee against Mrs. Danielson's fourth-grade class for spelling champion of the entire fourth grade, so this would be good practice.

Right away, I got excited. This essay, I knew, was a way for me to impress Mrs. Hunter with my maturity and exceptional writing skills.

Actually, my writing and spelling skills aren't all that exceptional (I'm better in math and science than I am in writing), but I figured at least I could write a really good essay that would make Mrs. Hunter forget about how many times she'd had to remind me not to chitchat with my neighbor (once since lunch).

So for my personal essay, I wrote:

My future goal is to be the best cat owner that I can possibly be when I adopt my kitten from the litter of Lady Serena Archibald, who is a purebred long-haired blue colorpoint Persian. I intend to name this kitten Mewsette (Mewsie for short — I am going to pick a girl kitten), and I will make sure that Mewsette is up-to-date on all of her vaccinations, has regular vet appointments, and when the time comes, I will make sure that Mewsette gets spayed so she doesn't have unwanted kittens herself. I will feed Mewsette only the best vet-recommended dry and wet food and make sure she always has fresh water (I already do this for our family dog, Marvin) and also clean out her litter box every single day.

I will also make sure that Mewsette gets her own bed, like the pink feathered canopy cat bed I saw in the pet store in the mall that is an almost exact copy of mine (only mine is for humans, not pets), and also that she gets the matching pink collar with genuine rhinestone trim I saw in the same store. The bed is only $49.99 and the collar is only $5.95, which I'm pretty sure my parents can afford. If not, I can do extra chores around the house such as clean the toilets, which is really my brother Mark's job, but I don't mind if it means my kitten can have the best, because she deserves it!

Actually, I went a little overboard on my essay, making it almost two pages, but I didn't think Mrs. Hunter would mind, because I was pretty sure the details about how I would earn the extra money to pay for Mewsette's bed and collar were important in describing my future goals.

I was reading over my essay and checking for spelling

errors when Mrs. Danielson, who teaches the fourth-grade class next door to ours (the one Prince Peter is in), opened the door to our classroom and said, "Mrs. Hunter, may I see you for a moment?" and Mrs. Hunter said, "Yes, of course."

Then she turned to our class and said, "Time's up, everyone. Would you please pass your essays to the left, and, Rosemary, would you please walk along the end of each row and gather everyone's papers and put them on my desk?"

Mrs. Hunter left the classroom to go out into the hall to talk to Mrs. Danielson while we passed our essays to the left. Rosemary got up and waited at the end of each row until she'd gathered all the essays.

But instead of putting them all on Mrs. Hunter's desk, like Mrs. Hunter had asked her to, Rosemary shuffled through the essays until she found one in particular. Then she began reading aloud from it in a babyish voice.

"'My future goal is to be the best cat owner that I can possibly be . . .'" Rosemary read, trying not to laugh. She was doing a better job than most of the class, who started laughing right away. They were laughing because Rosemary was making her voice all high and squeaky-sounding, like she was imitating someone. At first I couldn't figure out who she was trying to imitate, but a second later it became clear. "'. . . when I adopt my kitten from the litter of Lady Serena Archibald, who is a purebred long-haired blue colorpoint Persian. I intend to name this kitten Mewsette —'"

Me! Rosemary was imitating *me*! Did she think I really sounded like that? I do not sound like that. My voice is NOT that high and squeaky.

I could feel my cheeks turning bright red. But I was more mad than embarrassed this time. Because I knew I didn't really sound like that. Also, I knew my essay was good. I'd worked really hard on it. What was *her* essay about, anyway? Being mean to kids who were littler than she is while playing kick ball? Picking on the New Girl?

"Oh, ha-ha, Rosemary," I said, in a loud voice. *Standing up for yourself when others are being mean to you is important, especially when it's your first day of school.* That's a rule. Otherwise, it will set the tone for the whole year. "I thought Mrs.

Hunter said to put the essays on her desk, not read them."

"'Mewsette'!" Rosemary snorted. "That's the stupidest name for a cat!"

"I think it's cute," Erica said, trying, as always, to be the peacemaker.

"Yeah," Sophie said. "I like it!"

"'Mewsie for short'!" Rosemary said. She was still reading from my essay. She started using that funny voice again. "'I will also make sure that Mewsette gets her own bed, like the pink feathered canopy cat bed I saw in the pet store in the mall . . .'"

All of the boys were laughing now, especially the ones in the last row where Rosemary sat. A lot of the girls were laughing, too, but not all of them. Caroline, Sophie, and Erica weren't laughing, I noticed. Maybe they liked the name Mewsette. Or maybe they could see how red my face was, and maybe also that there were tears in my eyes.

Only I wasn't crying because I was upset. I was crying because I was so mad. I just couldn't believe how mean Rosemary was being! And that people thought she was funny! *It's never funny if someone's feelings are being hurt.* That's a rule.

Really, it's the most important rule of all.

"'. . . that is an almost exact copy of mine (only mine is for humans, not pets), and also that she gets the matching pink collar with genuine rhinestone trim I saw in the . . .'"

"ROSEMARY DAWKINS!"

Everyone's head, including Rosemary's, whipped around to see Mrs. Hunter standing in the doorway. Only Mrs. Hunter didn't look pretty and cool and fresh like she usually did. Mrs. Hunter looked as mad as I felt. Her cheeks were red, too, and her eyes were as bright as the silver stars she'd used to decorate her classroom with. She was staring at Rosemary so hard I wouldn't have been surprised if Rosemary's head exploded right in front of us and her brains splattered all around the classroom.

I wouldn't have minded if that happened, actually.

"Rosemary, what, exactly, do you think you're doing?" Mrs. Hunter demanded.

"Nothing," Rosemary said in a very small voice, putting the essays behind her back really fast. It was kind of hard to believe, but Rosemary looked scared.

Actually, I would have been scared, too, if Mrs. Hunter had been looking at *me* like that.

"When I ask you a question," Mrs. Hunter said, stepping toward Rosemary and holding out her hand for the essays, "I expect you to answer me honestly."

Rosemary had no choice but to hand over the essays. Mine was the first on the pile. Mrs. Hunter looked down at my essay. Then she looked over at me.

I guess Mrs. Hunter must have seen how upset I looked, since the next thing she asked was, "Allie, was Rosemary making fun of your essay?"

The thing is, I could have lied. I could have lied and said, *No, Mrs. Hunter, Rosemary wasn't making fun of my essay.*

This might have made Rosemary like me. Or hate me a little less, anyway.

But *You aren't supposed to lie to adults.* That's a rule. Not unless lying to them will make them feel better, like saying,

Oh, no, Uncle Jay, this microwaved Hot Pocket isn't frozen in the middle at all.

So I said, "Yes, Rosemary was making fun of my essay. I guess it's not the best essay in the world. But . . . I still didn't think it was very nice."

Because *that* was the truth.

"Whether it is the best essay in the world or not," Mrs. Hunter said, "in this classroom, we do not make fun of one another, and Rosemary knows that. That's why she's going to apologize to you. Aren't you, Rosemary?"

Rosemary, glaring at the floor, muttered something. Mrs. Hunter said, "I'm sorry, Rosemary, I didn't hear you."

"I'm sorry, Allie," Rosemary said in a louder voice.

"Thank you, Rosemary," Mrs. Hunter said. "And now, Rosemary, you can sit inside with me during afternoon recess and write another essay explaining the true meaning of friendship. The rest of you may get your coats now and line up to go outside."

We all went to the cloakroom to get our coats and lined

up for afternoon recess. All of us except Rosemary. Rosemary stayed exactly where she was, staring at the floor and looking very angry. I could tell she was angry and not sad because, even though her face was red, her eyebrows were hunched down, and she was frowning. It was pretty obvious Rosemary wanted to kill someone.

And you didn't have to be a genius to guess that the person she wanted to kill was me.

That's why I wasn't too surprised when, even though I tried really hard to stay out of her way when I was getting into the line on our way out to recess, I accidentally brushed past her and heard Rosemary whisper, "Allie, I'm going to beat you up later."

Because really, that was just pretty typical of the terrible day I was having.

RULE #4

When Someone Decides She's Going to Beat You Up, the Best Thing to Do Is Hide

The thing is, I've had girls hate me before. I've had girls so mad at me, they haven't spoken to me for *weeks*.

But none of them has ever actually threatened to beat me up. Mostly they just ignored me or said mean things about me behind my back or called me Allie Stinkle and stuff.

But Rosemary meant business. Erica told me she once beat up a kid named Morgan Hayes because Morgan ruined Rosemary's papier-mâché dragon in art class by accidentally sitting on it. So as revenge Rosemary sat on Morgan until Morgan cried.

And Morgan was a *boy*. And a *fifth-grader*.

When someone is going to beat you up, of course you have to take evasive action, such as Watching Your Back, Developing Eyes in the Back of Your Head, and basically Running and/or Hiding.

Fortunately, Rosemary took the bus home from school, so it wasn't like she could jump me from the bushes as I was walking home. If she tried this, she'd miss her ride and be stranded at Pine Heights Elementary overnight.

So the only place I really needed to worry about her was on the playground during morning, lunch, and afternoon recesses. The good thing was, as soon as Caroline, Sophie, and Erica heard what happened, they assured me they'd help me look out for her. Which was really, really nice of them.

And made me feel like, in spite of everything else that had happened, my first day at my new school hadn't been *that* bad, really. Having friends is a nice feeling. Even if none of them is a *best* friend.

"But really," Caroline said as we walked home from school, leaves crunching under our feet, "you should just tell Mrs. Hunter what Rosemary said."

"No, you shouldn't," Sophie said, shaking her head until her dark, glossy curls bounced. "That will just enrage her further. Like a monkey." Sophie, it turns out, is afraid of monkeys. Even though I assured her that monkeys rarely attack humans, as I know from the vast amount of reading I have done on the subject of mammals.

"Rosemary's not that bad," Erica the peacemaker said.

"I beg to differ," Sophie said. "Remember what she did to Morgan?"

"That's an urban myth," Caroline scoffed. "I heard he broke those ribs skiing when he was visiting his dad."

"Honestly," Erica said. "I think Rosemary was just letting off some steam. In a day or two she won't even remember she was mad. She doesn't have a good memory, anyway. Remember how long it took her to memorize the multiplication tables?"

"I don't know." Caroline looked dubious. "But I do know Mrs. Hunter isn't going to let someone in her own class get killed."

"But Mrs. Hunter can't be there all the time," Sophie reminded us all.

This was, sadly, very true.

Still, for a little while, anyway, avoiding Rosemary seemed to work. I started to think maybe Erica was right and that Rosemary had forgotten she was so mad at me. I was trying to be on my best behavior at school, not chit-chatting at *all* during class, not raising my hand to answer questions, being the last one in line to recess and to the music and art rooms, et cetera, so as not to draw attention to myself. In this way, I hoped that Rosemary would forget about my existence and, therefore, forget that she ever wanted to kill me.

And it seemed to be working. For a few days, she didn't even look at me. It helped, too, that Kevin had gotten over his desire to dress as a pirate, due to his impressive, rave-winning performance that first day and Mom's insistence that his costume was dirty and needed to be cleaned (and since it was Dry Clean Only, this meant it had to be taken to the cleaners). There was nothing to draw attention to me at school at all.

After what Mom called a rough start to my week (and I didn't even tell her about Rosemary. She just meant the thing with the popcorn for breakfast and wearing a skirt with jeans on my first day), things seemed to be going pretty well. Mom had even found the box with my leggings and tights in it, and Home Depot had called to say they'd located our stove. It wasn't due to arrive for another month, but at least they knew where it was. Things were looking up. I even got invited to a slumber party at Caroline's house! This was a very big deal, because it was the first slumber party I'd been to that wasn't with my friends from my old school.

And okay, it wasn't a huge slumber party. It was just me, Erica, Caroline, and Sophie.

But it was still super fun! We got to make dim sum, which are Chinese dumplings, with Caroline's dad's girl-friend, Wei-Lin.

Only it turns out you have to remember to wash your hands before you knead the dough, or it will turn out gray. But, like Wei-Lin said, oh, well, next time.

And despite what Sophie said, none of us got a stomach parasite from eating dirty dumpling dough, because if there were any parasites in it, they probably got baked.

So I was in a pretty good mood until I got home, and Mom greeted me at the door looking like she had some bad news.

"What?" I said. Because Mom only wore that expression when she had something to tell me and she didn't know quite how to break the news, like that we were out of Honey Nut Cheerios and I was going to have to eat the plain kind.

"Mrs. Hauser called while you were gone, honey," Mom said. Mrs. Hauser is the lady who owns Lady Serena Archibald.

"She did?" I threw down my sleeping bag and overnight case. I was pretty tired from my sleepover, even though it had been such a fun one. We'd stayed up most of the night watching DVDs and telling ghost stories. I don't like to brag, because *No one likes a braggart* (that's a rule), but my ghost stories, about a zombie hand, had been the scariest. Sophie told me she'd been so scared, she hadn't been able to sleep all night, thinking a zombie hand was going to come out of the attic in the night and strangle her.

Even though I told her there's no such thing as a zombie hand.

"They're worried Lady Serena Archibald is going to have the kittens too soon," Mom said. "Mrs. Hauser's taken her to the vet, and they're trying to see what they can do. But there's a chance Lady Serena might lose all the kittens — or maybe even die herself. Even if she does have them, they might be too young to survive. If they do survive, they'll need a lot of special care. Mrs. Hauser just wanted you to know. I'm so sorry, honey."

My eyes filled up with tears. I couldn't believe that while I'd been at Caroline's house, making dirty dim sum and telling ghost stories, Lady Serena Archibald, the mother of Mewsette, my kitten-to-be, had been maybe almost dying! Or losing Mewsette!

"I don't care how much special care Mewsette needs!" I yelled. "I'll do whatever it takes to keep her alive! I'm going to be a veterinarian anyhow, so it's never too early for me to start learning what I'll need to do."

"Allie, stop yelling," Mom said, looking more worried

than ever. "How will you look after a sick kitten while you're at school? A prematurely born kitten might need round-the-clock attention. You certainly can't stay up all night caring for it and also go to school."

"I can take Mewsette to school with me," I said. "My desk is big enough to keep a kitten inside. Mrs. Hunter will let me. I know she will!"

Mom looked more worried than ever. But I knew I was right. Mrs. Hunter was the nicest, prettiest teacher in the whole world. I knew she'd let me keep Mewsette with me in my desk at school all day. Maybe even in the pink feathered canopy cat bed I'd seen at the mall. Although I wasn't sure the bed would fit in my desk. In fact, I was pretty sure it wouldn't.

But maybe I could make a temporary bed for Mewsette out of a shoe box. A shoe box would fit. Or almost fit. I would be the only girl in the whole school with a sick newborn kitten in her desk. Everyone would see what a caring, nice person I was as I fed Mewsette from a bottle every hour, nursing her back to health. Even Rosemary would stop wanting to beat me up when she saw what a good nurse I was to a sick cat.

I ran over to Erica's house to tell her about Mewsette and see if she had any shoe boxes, because all the boxes in our house were huge, since we'd just moved, and had recently contained not one pair of shoes, but, like, twenty. Or a coffeemaker or set of golf clubs. Fortunately, Erica's sister, Melissa, had just bought a new pair of tap shoes (in addition to baton twirling, Missy is also an accomplished jazz and tap dancer), so we were able to spend the afternoon making a beautiful bed for Mewsette, even using a tiny velvet bag that used to hold a pair of Missy's earrings for Mewsette to rest her sweet precious little head on.

Only it turned out Missy hadn't really thrown out the velvet bag, and when she found out it was missing she came storming into Erica's room and ripped it out of the bed we'd made and called us a couple of ingrates and laughed cruelly at the idea of us ever nursing a sick premature kitten to health when we tried to explain, then stomped out again.

But Erica said to ignore her and that Melissa was always like that right before a twirling competition and that there was one coming up next week. I said I understood, even though I didn't. I knew Erica was just trying to keep the peace, like Caroline said she always does.

When we were done looking up the word "ingrate" in the dictionary and deciding that we aren't actually ungrateful or self-seeking, we went down into Erica's dining room and rang the secret bell under the dining table, which signals the maid in the kitchen (if Erica's family had a maid, but they don't. The bell is left over from olden times) until Erica's mom came out and told me it was time to go home.

I took the shoe box and went home and asked Mom if there was any more news from Mrs. Hauser, but there wasn't. By that time, we were all sitting down to a dinner of salad and microwaved macaroni and cheese, which we eat quite a lot, since we have no stove or oven. Also, Uncle Jay was visiting.

"Well," he said when we had all gathered at the table. "I have some interesting news."

"So do I," I said. "I'll go first. Lady Serena Archibald, the mother of my kitten-to-be, Mewsette, has gone into early labor and might die or have the kittens too soon, and they might be very sick, but that's okay, because as a future veterinarian, I'm prepared to nurse a premature kitten."

"No," Mom said. "Allie, that is not going to happen without some discussion first. That is too much responsibility for a nine-year-old girl. Jay, please tell us your news."

"Well," Uncle Jay said, "it's not quite as interesting as Allie's news, I'm afraid. But I spoke to Mom today — my mom, that is — and . . . well, kids . . . Grandma's coming!"

Mom laid down her fork with a bang.

Dad said, "Oh, yeah. I forgot. My mother is coming to visit next week."

"Yay!" Kevin yelled. "Grandma's coming! I hope she'll buy me a book about pirates!"

"I hope she'll buy me a dirt bike," Mark said.

"You just got a new mountain bike for your birthday," I reminded him.

"None of the kids in this neighborhood ride mountain bikes," Mark said. "They all ride dirt bikes. So I need a new bike."

"That's stupid," I said. "There's no difference between a dirt bike and a mountain bike."

"Uh," Mark said. "Excuse me. But there's a ton of difference."

"Uh," I said. "Excuse *me*. But you're wrong. And even if that's true, you don't need a whole new bike just to fit in. If your new friends don't like you the way you are, then they aren't really your friends."

"True," Mark said. "But I do need a whole new bike so I can do freestyle BMX racing or tricks."

Mom wasn't listening to our conversation, so she wasn't able to break in to say over her dead body was a son of hers going to become a freestyle BMX racer or trick performer.

"Your mother is coming to visit next week?" she asked Dad instead.

"She wants to see the new house," Dad said. "And the kids, of course."

"We don't have an oven," Mom said. "The bed in the guest room isn't set up. There aren't curtains in there."

"I'd offer to let her stay with me," Uncle Jay said, "but there's a reptile living in my spare bathroom."

"My mom's not picky," Dad said to Mom. "It's about visiting with family, not the luxury of the accommodations. Besides, she likes microwaved macaroni and cheese. Or she'll learn to like it, anyway."

"Why didn't you tell me you'd invited your mother to visit?" Mom asked Dad.

"I forgot," Dad said with a shrug. "Come on, it won't be that bad. It'll just be for a week."

"She can sleep in my bed," I said. "I can sleep in my sleeping bag on the floor. It will be easier to get up to nurse Mewsette there."

After dinner, Mom said she had a headache and had to go to bed early. Dad went upstairs to check on her. Uncle Jay helped me rinse the dishes and put them in the dishwasher while Mark and Kevin watched the half hour of family-friendly television we are allowed to view each night.

"So," Uncle Jay said. "A premature kitten. That's a lot of responsibility."

"Yes," I said. "And that's only if Lady Serena Archibald doesn't die. I sure hope she doesn't."

"If one life fails, another will take its place," Uncle Jay said, handing me a bunch of dripping silverware to put in the dishwasher. "At least with death comes a cessation of suffering."

"Whatever," I said. I was used to Uncle Jay's ramblings. "But I still really want a kitten."

"You'll still get a kitten," Uncle Jay said. "If it's meant to be. Lady Serena just may not be your kitten's mother."

But I really wanted Lady Serena to be my kitten's mom. I loved Lady Serena Archibald's long silky fur and the way she'd purr as she butted her head against your hand if you held it out to her. Surely her kittens would have the same sort of fur and do the same thing with their heads. I really, really hoped Lady Serena would be okay.

But Mrs. Hauser didn't call. And I couldn't ask Mom to call her, because Mom had gone to bed early.

It was hard to sleep that night because I kept thinking

about Lady Serena and praying that she would be okay. In the morning when I woke up, it was almost as if I hadn't gotten any sleep whatsoever. I felt super draggy, and I didn't feel like going to school at all. What did school matter when a cat was possibly dying?

Maybe it was because I was so tired that I didn't remember until Erica reminded me on the way to school that it was the day of the big fourth-grade spelling bee, when Mrs. Hunter's fourth-grade class was competing against Mrs. Danielson's fourth-grade class for spelling champion of our grade. I am not the world's greatest speller under the best of circumstances . . .

. . . but I guess I had studied a little, looking up the word "ingrate," and all.

Still, I didn't have much faith I was going to perform very well, given how little sleep I'd had and how worried I was over Lady Serena.

Caroline, Sophie, and Erica tried to comfort me, but there really wasn't very much they could say or do, even though it was nice of them to try — especially Caroline, because she didn't feel too well on account of having eaten way too many of Mrs. Harrington's chocolate-chocolate chip cookies that Erica had brought over for the slumber party (Sophie suggested maybe Caroline's stomachache was because of a parasite in the dirty dumpling dough, but I pointed out that none of the rest of us were sick, and Caroline *had* eaten about thirty of those cookies. Even Sophie had to agree this was true).

I just couldn't get the picture of beautiful Lady Serena, with her long silver-blue fur, lying on a veterinary hospital gurney with an oxygen mask over her little cat nose, panting for breath, out of my head. If only I knew whether or not she was going to be okay!

It was hard enough to pay attention during my first class, math, what with wondering whether I was going to get a baby kitten after all. But then there was the anticipation of the spelling bee, which caused everyone to keep glancing at the clock. It was going to be held down in the gym because that was the only room big enough for both fourth-grade classes. Everyone was waiting for Mrs. Hunter to say, "Okay, class. It's time to line up." Some people in the class — like Rosemary, who actually liked competition (unlike me. *It's never fun when somebody loses and ends up cry-ing . . . that's a rule*) — couldn't wait, they were so excited. They kept whispering things like, "We're going to smear Danielson's class" and "Caroline's going to win. Wait and see," because Caroline had won the third-grade spelling bee last year.

Which was good. I was glad I was friends with the girl who was going to win. And it took some of the pressure off me. Even though I don't like competition, I sure didn't want to be in the *losing* class. Or be the person who caused our class to lose.

And then before I knew it Mrs. Hunter was saying, "All right, class. It's time. I hope you're ready," which I most definitely was not (if Mom and Dad would just let me have a cell phone, I could have called them to see if they'd heard anything about Lady Serena Archibald, and then I'd have known how she was doing and I wouldn't have been so nervous. Why won't they let me get a cell phone? It's so unfair).

We all got into our lines and Mrs. Hunter started lead-ing us down the stairs to the gym. On the way, we ran into

Mrs. Danielson's class, who were also going down to the gym. Even though we aren't supposed to talk when we're in our lines, I heard Rosemary go "We're going to *kill you*" to Mrs. Danielson's class. "See this girl?" Rosemary pointed to Caroline. "She's going to knock you down and wipe you up *like a mop*."

I wondered if Mrs. Danielson's class was as scared as I'd been when Rosemary had told me she was going to beat me up. She hadn't mentioned this to me in a while, but I knew this was only because she'd temporarily forgotten about me. Pretty soon I'd probably do something to remind Rosemary that she wanted to knock *me* down and wipe me up like a mop. It was really only a matter of time.

Still, Mrs. Danielson's class didn't look that scared. They trooped over to the chairs that Mr. Elkhart, the custodial arts manager, had set up for us to sit in, on their side of the gym, while we sat in the ones he'd set up for our class. Everyone was nervously talking and giggling, especially when we saw the neat row of ten chairs lined up beneath the basketball net in front of the stage and near the entrance to the gym. I asked Erica what those chairs were for, and she said, "They're for the ten finalists."

I said, "Oh." I really hoped I wouldn't mess up if I got to be one of the ten finalists and I was standing in front of everyone. Especially if I was standing in front of Rosemary.

It was only then that Caroline whispered to me, "Allie, I don't know if I can win this time. I'm really not feeling well."

I whispered back, "Is it the cookies?"

Caroline, looking miserable, nodded. I swallowed hard. I couldn't believe it. If Caroline didn't win the spelling bee for our class, someone was going to get knocked down and wiped up like a mop.

And I had a feeling that someone wasn't going to be in Mrs. Danielson's class. It was going to be the kid from our class who missed the last word.

I for sure didn't want that kid to be me.

That's when the spelling bee started. Mrs. Hunter and Mrs. Danielson took turns going down the rows asking kids to spell different words. To be fair, Mrs. Danielson took the kids from Mrs. Hunter's class, and Mrs. Hunter took the kids from Mrs. Danielson's class, so no kid had an unfair advantage of being asked words the teacher knew that he or she would get right. If a kid got a word right, then he or she stood up. If he or she got the word wrong, then he or she sat down and was out of the bee. That's how it would get down to the final ten kids who would stand up in front of the whole gym.

Already Mrs. Danielson's class was down four people and Mrs. Hunter's class was down five when it was my turn. My heart was beating so hard when Mrs. Danielson got to me, I thought I was going to throw up. *Let it be an easy word,* I prayed. *Easy word, easy word.* Really, I had way more to worry about already than letting down my class. I mean, why me? I was maybe already the stepmother of a premature kitten! I didn't need to lose a spelling bee on top of that already very stressful worry!

"Horse," Mrs. Danielson said. "Allie, your word is 'horse.'"

Oh, my gosh, could I have gotten an easier word? Really, I have been reading books about horses since the first grade. I stood up and was confidently about to spell "horse" when I glanced at Caroline and saw her eyebrows sloped downward in concern. Wait a second . . . why did Caroline look so worried? Everyone knew how to spell "horse." Mark, in the second grade, could spell "horse." What was the big deal?

Then I remembered. There were two different versions of the word "horse."

Wow! I had almost missed my very first word, and because of an easy mistake!

"Could you use the word in a sentence, please?" I asked.

"Your voice is sounding very hoarse today," Mrs. Danielson said.

Whoa! I had almost spelled the wrong version! I would have missed and been out because of a silly mistake! Good thing I'd looked at Caroline!

"Hoarse," I said. "H-O-A-R-S-E. Hoarse."

"Very good," Mrs. Danielson said, smiling. "You may remain standing."

I glanced over at Mrs. Hunter and saw her give me a big smile. Phew! I hadn't let down the class. I sneaked a glance at Rosemary. She didn't exactly smile at me, but she didn't look like she wanted to kill me, either. I didn't really get to see what she thought, though, because Sophie, who was standing on the other side of me from Erica, nudged me and whispered, "Look!"

I looked and saw that it was Prince Peter's turn, over on Mrs. Danielson's side of the gym. He stood up and, looking handsome in a green sweater, correctly spelled the word "urgent."

"Like my love for him," Sophie whispered to me. "It's very *urgent*."

Then we both started to giggle, until Mrs. Danielson looked over in our direction and said, "Girls," in a stern voice. And we both stopped laughing right away. I'm so glad Mrs. Hunter is our teacher and not her. It must be terrible to have a teacher that old, with a neck that wobbles so much. I would cry every single day if Mrs. Danielson was my teacher.

The spelling bee kept going until soon there were more people sitting down than standing up — and I was one of them! Sophie got knocked out on "excite" — which is a hard word — and Erica missed on "embarrass"— also really hard. I only got "embarrass" right because I guessed after hearing Erica spell it wrong with one "r." Then later I got "wallaby," which is a type of macropod, otherwise known as a kangaroo or wallaroo. Really, it isn't fair to give me any type of animal word because I've read every book in the library about them, and I went through an extreme kangaroo phase in the second grade.

Then the next thing I knew, I was in the final ten! I couldn't believe it! Suddenly, I was walking up to stand in front of both fourth-grade classes, with Caroline and one other kid from our class, a boy named Lenny Hsu. That was it! We were the only ones left from Mrs. Hunter's class! Everyone else in the final ten, including Peter Jacobs, was from Mrs. Danielson's class.

Caroline, I could tell, really wasn't feeling well. She was sweating, and her face looked a little green. I couldn't believe that a full day after eating all those cookies, she was still sick. Although she *had* eaten an awful lot of them. Mrs. Harrington is a terrific baker.

And sure enough, two words after Lenny had to sit down because he misspelled "mischief," Mrs. Danielson gave Caroline the word "geriatric," and she was out.

I wasn't the only person who couldn't believe it. You could tell that everyone in the whole gym was stunned. The champion speller, out on such an easy word? It wasn't even a sixth- or seventh-grade word. "Geriatric" was a fifth-grade word! And Caroline Wu had missed it! No one could understand what had happened.

No one except those of us who knew about Mrs. Harrington's chocolate-chocolate chip cookies, of course.

Now I was the only person from Mrs. Hunter's class standing in the front of the gym — me and Prince Peter. The pressure was just too much! I knew I was going to crack. Because *When the mother of your kitten is at the veterinary hospital in premature labor, and you don't know if you're going to get a cat or not, and a girl in your class says she's going to beat you up, and you know if you mess up, she's going to do it for* sure, *it's hard to concentrate on spelling.*

That's a rule.

But maybe I was wrong. Maybe I'd do okay. Maybe Mrs. Danielson would give me the word "ingrate," and I would spell it correctly, and I would win the spelling bee for our class, and everyone would lift me onto their shoulders and carry me around, cheering, and people at Pine Heights Elementary would stop considering me the New Girl . . .

. . . and Rosemary Dawkins wouldn't want to kill me anymore.

It could happen.

RULE #5

Friends — and Queens — Don't Let Each Other Get Beaten Up

Except it totally didn't.

What happened instead was all the kids in Mrs. Hunter's class, out in the audience in the gym, led by Rosemary, were totally making me super nervous every time I got a word by chanting my name like I was a football player or something. They kept going, "AL-LIE! AL-LIE!"

And that wasn't actually helping. That was actually doing the opposite of helping. It was making me *more* nervous. Like, it was making my hands start to sweat and making me want to go out into the hallway to get a drink of water.

Only you couldn't go out into the hallway to get a drink of water. Because this was the fourth-grade spelling bee, and it was serious. Our class had to win, or we'd be completely humiliated. Also, Rosemary Dawkins might kill me.

But all I could think about was that at this very moment, Lady Serena Archibald might actually be dying. Really, literally, *dying*. And I didn't even know it. I was at school in a stupid spelling bee. What did knowing how to spell words even matter? When I was a grown-up I would have a computer at my job like my mom and dad, anyway, and that computer would have a spell-checker on it. So why did I even need to know how to spell?

Plus, I want to be a veterinarian, like the one who was hopefully saving Lady Serena's life right now. How did knowing how to spell help you to be a better veterinarian?

It was right then that Mrs. Danielson said, "Allie? Are you ready?" and I realized it was my turn again.

I couldn't believe it! Already? It felt like it had just been my turn. Hadn't I spelled "anarchy"? I was so tired from getting no sleep from staying up all night worrying, plus from telling ghost stories for hours the night before.

But just like last time, Rosemary was leading all the boys who sat in the last row with her in Mrs. Hunter's class in chiming, "AL-LIE! AL-LIE!" The whole class, I knew, was counting on me. Me, the New Girl. I couldn't let them down.

"Allie," Mrs. Danielson said. "Your word is 'doctor.' 'Doctor.'"

I wiped my sweat-soaked hands on my jeans, feeling relieved. Doctor! That was easy.

"Doctor," I said. "D-O-C-T —"

Wait. Wait a minute. Was it E-R? Or O-R? I couldn't remember. I was so tired. Doctor? Or docter? They both sounded right. Which *was* it?

It had to be E-R. Because that's where doctors work. In an ER. ER stands for emergency room. So it had to be D-O-C-T-E-R.

I glanced over at Caroline for support in the audience . . . but she wasn't there anymore. She had been led out to go to the nurse's office. Maybe they'd have to take her to the ER.

It had to be E-R. It just *had* to . . .

"E-R," I finished.

"That is incorrect," Mrs. Danielson said.

What? Oh, no!

Mrs. Hunter's entire fourth-grade class groaned . . . but none so loudly as Rosemary.

That was it. I was dead. Again.

Keeping my head down, my gaze glued to my shoes, I slunk back to my seat, barely comforted by the pats Erica and Sophie gave me as I sat down.

"It's all right," Erica said. "I thought it was spelled that way, too."

But that didn't make me feel better. Especially when I risked a glance over my shoulder and saw Rosemary staring right at me, her eyes narrowed in a way that let me know that as soon as the spelling bee was over, I was a dead woman.

The spelling bee ended as soon as Prince Peter spelled "doctor" correctly (it was O-R, after all. Which makes sense, because doctors operate in an operating room called an OR). So Mrs. Danielson's class was the one that got to celebrate. And Rosemary hated me more than ever, as was quickly proved when we were going out the gym doors to head upstairs to get our coats before walking home for lunch, and Rosemary leaned over and hissed, "I'm still going to kill you, Finkle. Don't think I forgot. Because I haven't."

Caroline, who was standing nearby, having been let out of the nurse's office, overheard her and gave me a serious look.

"Allie." She came over to me to whisper. "You *have* to tell Mrs. Hunter. If you won't, *I* will."

"No," I said. "It's okay. Really. I have it all under control."

Caroline gave me a weird look, like, *What are you talking about? No, you don't.*

But the last thing I wanted was Mrs. Hunter getting involved and punishing Rosemary again. That would only get Rosemary even *more* mad at me.

Of course, *Pretending like you have things under control and actually* having *things under control are two very different things* (this is a rule). This was made all too clear to us when we were filing out to lunch and Peter Jacobs walked up while I was heading downstairs with Sophie, Caroline, and Erica.

"Hi," Peter said to me. "I just wanted to say that I hope there's no hard feelings. I didn't think you'd strike out on something as easy as the word 'doctor,' Allie."

I felt my cheeks getting hot. I couldn't believe Prince Peter knew my name! But I guess it wasn't any big surprise, seeing how the class had been chanting it and all. I threw a glance at Sophie and saw that her face was as pink as I knew mine was probably turning.

"The mother of Allie's future kitten is really sick," Erica told Peter quickly. "She's really worried about her. She's in the cat hospital!"

"Oh," Peter said, his expression going from teasing to concerned. "I'm really sorry. No wonder you had a hard time with a word like 'doctor.' I hope she gets better soon."

"Thanks, Pr — I mean, Peter," I said.

Oh, my gosh! I almost called him *Prince* Peter! Beside me, I could hear Sophie trying not to burst into giggles. I had to keep my gaze on the ground to prevent myself from doing the same thing. Fortunately, Peter went away before we collapsed against each other in hysterical laughter.

"What's so funny?" Kevin wanted to know, coming over to meet us so we could walk him home.

"Didn't you hear what she said?" Sophie asked, wiping laugh tears from her eyes.

"Never mind," Caroline said, taking Kevin's hand. "Come on. Let's get you home."

"Awwww," Kevin said, sad that he wasn't being let in on the secret.

"That was nice of Peter to say that about Lady Serena," Erica said as we walked out of the school.

"Yes," I said. I couldn't really feel too good about Peter's niceness, though, because it was in such sharp contrast with Rosemary's meanness. I mean, the part about how she was waiting to kill me. Plus, I was still worrying about the whole Lady-Serena-maybe-probably-dying part.

When I got home for lunch, though, and was hanging up my coat, Mom came into the mudroom off the garage (which is where she'd decided we kids needed to start coming into the house, now that she knew Grandma was coming to visit at the end of the month. She was hoping it would keep some of our mess contained in one place) and said, "Allie, I just got off the phone with Mrs. Hauser."

I swear, I think my heart must have skipped *two* beats at this news.

"And?" I asked, hoping my prayers had been answered and I hadn't done all that worrying for nothing.

"And this morning at the vet's office Lady Serena gave birth to six kittens," Mom said.

I caught my breath. Six baby kittens! "Oh!"

"But," Mom went on, a serious look on her face, "before you get too excited, they were born way, way too early, and the doctor isn't sure that they're all going to make it."

"Oh," I said in a different tone of voice, my hopes all fading.

"On the bright side," Mom said, "Lady Serena is going to be all right. That's really what matters to Mrs. Hauser. She's too small a cat to have been carrying that many kittens."

Well, that was true. Lady Serena was a very fragile, lady-like cat.

"Do you think," I asked, following Mom into the kitchen, where she was making our lunch of microwaved chicken noodle soup and cheese and crackers, "I could go over to the animal hospital to see the kittens? And Lady Serena, too, of course?"

"Oh, no, honey," Mom said. "Mrs. Hauser said Lady Serena is in intensive care."

I couldn't help feeling more worried than ever. How was I going to be able to choose my kitten? Mrs. Hauser had promised me first pick from the litter. I know it was selfish to be thinking that when they were still so little and sick.

But when I mentioned this out loud, Mom said, "Oh, honey, the kittens are still too tiny to even have opened their eyes. Mrs. Hauser says they're completely hairless."

"Like newts," Mark said cheerfully.

"Shut up," I said. I was really, really mad at him all of a sudden. "Kittens are nothing like newts."

"They are when they're that little," Mark said. "And have no hair."

"They are not," I insisted. "Mom, make Mark stop it."

"Mark, stop teasing your sister," Mom said. "Allie, you're just going to have to be patient about your kitten. Mrs. Hauser is doing the best she can in a bad situation. Now sit down and eat. How was school today so far?"

"Allie lost the fourth-grade spelling bee," Kevin said conversationally as he shoveled cheese and crackers into his face. "In front of everyone. And a boy named Peter talked to her."

Fortunately, Kevin didn't know anything about Rosemary wanting to kill me. He hadn't overheard *that* part of the conversation. What little he'd said upset Mom enough. It's important that, when they ask, you tell your parents some stuff about what happened in school that day. But not *everything*. Because sometimes if you tell them everything, they call your teacher and complain, and that could make everything even worse. This had actually happened to me one time when a kid in second grade kept trying to kiss me on the playground at recess (later I figured out it was because he liked me. Ew. Also, *ew*). I told my mom and she called the kid's mom and his mom took away his PlayStation to punish him and he was so mad about it that at recess he came up and knocked over the stick village I had made for the invisible people who lived in the dirt (I was very immature in the second grade and thought invisible people lived in the dirt on the playground).

So *You have to be careful what you tell your mom. At least if she's the kind of mom who is just going to make things worse,* like my mom sometimes does.

This a rule.

Finally, Mom got done fussing over my losing the spelling bee in front of everyone and let me go so I could meet Erica outside. We walked slowly back to school together, shuffling through the dead leaves, while I told her about Lady Serena. Erica agreed it was unfair that I wasn't allowed to go to the animal hospital to see how Lady Serena was doing. I am actually extremely good around animals. I am the only one in our family who takes care of Marvin, our dog, except for Dad, who walks him. My help could totally be invaluable to the vet technicians. I once took a nail out of Marvin's paw pad. True, it hadn't been in that deep, but if left inside, it could have festered and caused an infection. How could Mom not have remembered?

We met Sophie and Caroline by the stop sign at the corner, where she and Caroline turned off to go to their houses. Caroline said she felt a lot better now that her dad had given her some medicine for her stomach and that she was sorry she had let us all down. Sophie said the real problem wasn't Caroline and her losing the spelling bee to Prince Peter but what we were going to do about Allie and Rosemary.

"What?" I said as innocently as I could. "There's no problem with Rosemary."

"Allie," Caroline said, "she's totally going to want to kill you after this. You lost the spelling bee for our class. You know how competitive she is."

"We're just going to have to figure out a way to protect Allie," Erica said firmly. "That's what queens do for one another. Right?"

"Us?" Sophie said. She looked a little scared. "How are we going to do that? I mean . . . Rosemary's way bigger than we are. Not to mention stronger."

"Not if we stick together," Caroline said. "Erica's right. We just have to be Allie's bodyguards and never leave her alone for a second on the playground. Rosemary won't dare try anything if we're around and can run for Mrs. Hunter."

"You guys," I said, touched by this gesture. Really. My heart swelled with love for them. I couldn't believe how sweet they were being, especially considering I was just the New Girl. They had to be the best friends I had ever had. Even if none of them had officially declared themselves my best friend. "You don't have to do that."

"Yes, we do," Caroline said. "That's what friends are for."

"And queens," Erica said. "Don't forget queens."

Sophie nodded, although she still looked a little scared. "It's true," she said.

I almost started to cry, I thought this was so nice of them. Because it really is true:

Friends — and queens — don't let each other get beaten up.

That's totally a rule.

RULE #6

Peaceful, Nonviolent Conflict Resolution Is Always the Answer

Even though Caroline, Sophie, and Erica said they'd be my bodyguards, they couldn't be around to protect me from Rosemary Dawkins and the death warrant she'd taken out against me *all* the time.

They couldn't be there, for instance, when Mrs. Hunter gave me a note to take down to Mrs. Jenkins, the principal, and I was coming back up the stairs and ran into Rosemary as she was coming out of the girls' room.

A part of me thought maybe she'd gotten the bathroom pass and was *waiting* for me in the girls' room.

But another part of me was, like, no way Rosemary hated me enough to do that.

Still, when I came up the stairs, totally minding my

own business, Rosemary was, like, "Oh, hey, *loser.* There you are, *loser.*"

I looked all around the hallway, wondering who Rosemary could have been talking to. But the only other person there was Mr. Elkhart, the custodial arts manager, who was mopping up some of Morgan Hayes's throw-up from earlier in the day. I didn't think Rosemary could be calling Mr. Elkhart a loser, because *It isn't polite to call adults names.* That's a rule.

I guess it was lucky for me Mr. Elkhart *was* there, though, because Rosemary didn't push me down and start whaling on me right then and there or anything, since he was leaning on his mop, watching us. I just went, "Hey, Rosemary," and made a big wide circle around her so she couldn't reach me if she swung out her fist.

Still, even though she couldn't hit me, Rosemary could tease me. So she did, by going, "Whatcha so scared of, huh, scaredy-cat? Huh? Are you an alley cat or a scaredy-cat?"

I just kept walking back into our classroom, because Mrs. Hunter had only given me permission to take her note down to Mrs. Jenkins's office, not hang around in the hallway and talk to Rosemary. When I got back to my seat and Erica saw Rosemary come in right behind me and lay her bathroom pass on Mrs. Hunter's desk, she turned her head real fast to look at me, like, *Are you all right?*

But I opened my English book to the page we were all on and made myself look super busy and didn't say anything to anyone about it (especially since we aren't supposed to chitchat with our neighbor during class time) until recess, when I told Erica, Sophie, and Caroline about it in the safety of our pretend castle behind the bushes on the playground.

"Something has to be done to stop her," Sophie said.

"Yeah," Caroline said. "We should tell Mrs. Hunter."

"NO!" I cried at the same time as Sophie.

"That will only enrage her further," Sophie explained.

"There has to be another way," Erica said.

"What if Allie learned self-defense?" Sophie asked.

"What's that?" Erica wanted to know.

"The art of defending oneself against one's enemies," Caroline said. "And I'd like to register my disapproval.

Peaceful, nonviolent conflict resolution is always the answer."

That sounded good. That sounded, in fact, like it should be a rule.

Except nobody else seemed to think so.

"My older brother showed it to me once," Sophie said. "He knows all the most painful places on the human body to register a kick, and I think if Allie just drove her heel into the arch of Rosemary's foot, she'd disable her long enough to run for help. And that's really the best strategy in this situation."

"What if Rosemary's wearing boots?" Erica wanted to know.

"Her inner thigh, then," Sophie said.

"I can't kick anybody," I said, horrified. I mean, I kick my little brothers all the time when one of them won't surrender the remote. Not *hard* or anything, but to give them a gentle reminder that *I am the oldest child and so I am the one in charge.* This is obviously a rule. But sometimes they forget.

But I have never kicked a stranger, or even an acquaintance who was not actually related to me. Once, I kicked my cousin Todd. But he is my own age, and also, he completely deserved it for saying our house was old. And that wasn't even our new house, it was our old house, which was a contemporary split-level and was built in this century so he didn't know what he was talking about. And he didn't even cry, so it wasn't that hard a kick or anything.

"You're probably going to have to kick Rosemary," Sophie said. "Because if you don't kick her, she's going to punch your lights out. Kicking her, then running away is your only chance at survival. I wish there were some other way."

"I'm sorry," Caroline said. "But violence of any kind is wrong, and responding to Rosemary's violence with violence of your own is *especially* wrong."

"How come it's not wrong when we're playing queens and chopping off the heads of evil warlords?" Sophie asked her.

"Because that," Caroline said, "is pretend. Allie could really get hurt doing this."

As if I didn't know this! Also, if Caroline was so concerned about me, where had she been during the spelling bee, when I really could have used her support? I know she'd felt sick, but fewer cookies and a little more spelling skill would have been helpful.

"All we're saying Allie should do is incapacitate her enemy, then run for help," Sophie explained to Caroline.

"What's 'incapacitate'?" Erica asked.

"You know," Sophie said. "Prevent Rosemary from functioning normally for a moment because she's busy writhing in pain."

"Oh, dear," Erica said. "I guess so, then."

"I don't know." Caroline looked doubtful.

I kind of agreed with Caroline. I thought incapacitating Rosemary, just like telling Mrs. Hunter, was only going to make Rosemary madder. The whole situation, really, was turning out to be one where no matter what I did, it seemed like it was going to get me beat up worse than if I continued to do what I was doing now . . . which was nothing.

Ultimately, I could see I was going to have to consult with someone who actually had experience in this kind of thing, since it didn't look as if the situation was going to improve on its own.

And I knew exactly whom to go to.

I found my dad putting together the bed (with Mark's help) in the guest bedroom after school, in preparation for Grandma's visit at the end of the week. Dad had just said a bunch of swear words because while he is very good at teaching college kids how to write computer programs, he is not very good at putting beds together. When you say a bad word in our house, you are supposed to pay a quarter. When we get enough quarters, we take Marvin to the dog grooming place and he gets a shampoo and comb out and comes back looking beautiful. Until he rolls in the dirt, which he usually does the first chance he gets, because he doesn't like the way the dog shampoo smells.

I pretended I didn't hear Dad's swears, though, because I wanted to talk to him about something serious.

"Dad," I said, "how do you fight someone?"

Mark started laughing, although I didn't really see what was so funny.

"Fight someone?" Dad was putting a screw into the bed frame he was assembling. He had the screw he was going to use in his mouth so he wouldn't lose it, so he was talking kind of funny. "Why do you want to fight someone?"

"I don't *want* to fight anybody," I said. "Somebody wants to fight me."

"Who wants to fight you?" Mark wanted to know. Mark was holding the nut so Dad wouldn't lose it.

"Nobody," I said. *The less your little brothers know about your business, the better off you are.* That's a rule. A big one.

"The best way to fight someone," Dad said, taking the screw from his mouth and putting it in the hole, "is to punch them in the nose."

"Why the nose?" I asked.

"Because," Dad said while Mark held the nut in place, "it really hurts to get punched in the nose. But the nose is only made up of cartilage, which splinters easily beneath the knuckles, and so you won't hurt your hand punching it. As opposed to if you punch the guy in his mouth — then you'd cut your knuckles on his teeth. Or in the jaw or the eye — you'd bruise your knuckles on bone."

"Gee, Dad," Mark said admiringly. "You must have hit a lot of guys, huh?"

"Oh, no," Dad said. "I just got beat up a lot in school."

I looked down at my fists. I didn't think I could punch Rosemary. For one thing, she was a lot taller than me. I wasn't sure I could reach her face.

"No, no, no," Dad said, noticing what I was doing. "That's not how you make a fist. Here."

He put down the partially made bed frame and stood up and came over to me.

"First of all," Dad said, "never put your thumb inside your fingers when you make a fist. Because when you hit someone, you'll only end up breaking your thumb. Keep your thumb outside. Like this."

Dad showed me how to make a fist, keeping my thumb outside my fist. Mark came over to show me, as well, even though I'm pretty sure Mark's never been in a fight in his life. Except with me. But the only fights we've been in I've always won by sitting on top of him and then threatening to spit in his face. This is an excellent way to win fights with your brothers. But only if they are smaller than you are.

"That's right," Dad said. "Now, try punching me in the middle of the hand." He held up his big open palm.

"No, Dad," I said, lowering my fist. "I can't."

"Yes, you can," Dad said. He tapped the middle of his palm. "Right here, as hard as you can."

I didn't want to punch my dad. I didn't want to punch *anyone!*

On the other hand, though, I didn't want to *get* punched, either. So if it was a choice between learning to punch and getting punched . . .

I pulled my arm back and punched the center of my dad's palm, not as hard as I could, because I didn't want to hurt him. His hand didn't even move. But my fist bounced right off.

Mark laughed.

"That was all right," Dad said, giving Mark a disapproving look for laughing. "But I think you could do better."

I glared at Mark. I couldn't believe he'd laughed. I'd like to see how hard he'd try to hit his own father.

"Tell me about this guy who wants to fight you. What'd you do to him? Call him a name or something?"

"It's not a guy," I said. "It's a girl."

"A girl?" Dad looked surprised. "I didn't know girls fought. I mean, physically."

"Oh, they fight," I assured him. As I said it, my stomach gave a twist, the way it always did when I thought about Rosemary. "She says she's going to kill me."

"Well," Dad said, "pretend you're not hitting me. Pretend you're punching her." He held up his hand again. "Now hit me. And don't hit with just your arm. Throw your whole body behind the punch."

"Dad," I said uncomfortably.

"Do it, Allie," Dad said.

"Just do it, Allie," Mark said. "Really whale on him."

I took a deep breath. Then I closed my eyes. I

remembered how scared I'd been in that hallway when it had been just me and Rosemary (until I'd noticed Mr. Elkhart). Then I opened my eyes and punched my dad's hand, throwing my whole body behind the punch.

"Ow," Dad said, waving his hand in the air like it stung. "Good one, Allie."

"Yeah, that was good, Allie," Mark said. "Did you hear that cracking sound? I think that was Dad's hand bones. Right, Dad?"

"That's enough practicing for today," Dad said. "You've got your technique down. Let's talk strategy."

"Strategy?" I asked.

"Yeah," Dad said. He wrapped the hand I'd punched around the cup of coffee he'd been drinking. "When is this fight going to go down?"

"I don't know," I said. "Whenever she jumps me. It's her choice. She's a lot bigger than me."

"A *fifth*-grader wants to kill you?" Mark asked, looking impressed.

I didn't want him to know the truth, especially since he knew Rosemary. I mean, he played kick ball with her every day at recess. I wasn't sure he especially liked her. Rosemary, unlike Prince Peter, was pretty mean to the kids who were littler than she was. But Mark was a tough kid, so he probably didn't even notice.

Still, I ignored his question. "What if I can't reach her nose?"

"A punch in the gut should make her double over," Dad said, looking thoughtful, "and then you'll be able to land one on her nose. But, you know, maybe this is something you should talk to your mother about."

"No!" I said, and Mark nodded.

"Mom'll just call Allie's teacher," Mark explained, "and the teacher'll say something to the kid, and the kid'll know Allie told, and then she'll want to kill Allie even more, for being a tattletale."

I threw Mark a grateful look. The truth is, even though little brothers can be a pain sometimes, other times they can be nice to have around because they know exactly what you are thinking and feeling. Because they are thinking and feeling the same thing.

"She'll wait until no one is around," Mark went on, "and

then when Allie least expects it, she'll come jumping out from the shadows, and *WHAM!*"

Other times, though, little brothers go just one step too far.

"So Allie better know what to do," Mark concluded.

Dad looked thoughtful. "Right," he said. "But, you know, your mother wouldn't approve of fighting."

"But, Dad," I said, "Mark's right. Whether or not Mom approves, I have to know how to defend myself, right? Because she's not going to be able to protect me twenty-four hours a day."

"Still," Dad said. Now he looked uncomfortable. "I —"

I gulped. "What's that?" I said. "I think I hear Mom calling. I better go downstairs and see what she wants."

I ran out of the room. I didn't really hear Mom calling, of course. I made that part up. I just didn't want to think about what Rosemary might do to me if Dad told Mom what was going on, and Mom called Mrs. Hunter, and Mrs. Hunter said something to her about it. I walked into the kitchen just as Mom was hanging up the phone.

"Good news," Mom said.

I didn't think the news could be that Rosemary Dawkins had been picked to star in her own Disney series and was moving to Hollywood and I'd never have to see her again. I knew that would be too much to hope for.

"That was Mrs. Hauser on the phone just now," Mom said. "Lady Serena and the kittens are doing so well the veterinary hospital is sending them home. Mrs. Hauser says Lady Serena has finally started feeding them and caring for them, and in a few days, they should start growing fur and opening their eyes. And then you'll be able to go over and pick the one that you want — though they'll still need to stay with their mother for a few more weeks until they're weaned."

I just stood there, so shocked I didn't know what to say. What with all the bad news I'd been having lately, I couldn't believe there was actually a piece of good news!

"Is there a striped one?" I asked her. "An adorable gray-and-black-striped one with a white belly and white socks on its feet?"

"I don't know," Mom said. "Like Mrs. Hauser just said, none of them has any fur yet. They're hairless, like newts."

"Stop saying they're like newts," I shouted. "Baby kittens don't look anything like newts! Newts are slimy and green! Baby kittens are cute!"

"There's no need to shout, Allie," Mom said. "I have enough problems, with your father springing this visit from Grandma on me."

"Visits from Grandma are fun," I said, surprised. "She always brings us stuff."

"Yeah," Mom said, popping open the freezer, since our stove still hadn't arrived. Tonight we were having salad and frozen French bread pizzas. I was going to have to peel the cheese off mine and scrape all the tomato sauce off, since one of my rules is *Never eat anything red.* "Right. I just don't exactly have this house ready for visitors yet."

"Well, Dad's got the bed ready." We both listened as a few more swears floated down from upstairs. "Almost," I added.

"The truth is, Allie," Mom said, with a sigh, "this house is never going to be ready enough for your grandmother."

I didn't know what Mom meant by that.

I got to find out when Grandma arrived later that week, though.

RULE #7

Ask Old People What to Do Because They Know Everything

I managed to avoid Rosemary — and having to punch her in the stomach, and then the nose — by never venturing out onto the playground at recess by myself. I always had my queens with me. For some reason, Rosemary wasn't willing to beat me up when other people were around, watching. I wasn't sure why.

Although I suspected it was because she didn't want any witnesses who could testify against her. I saw that in a movie once.

Just as things sort of started looking up, Mrs. Hunter made the announcement that there was going to be a special all-star finalist spelling bee. The final ten from the fourth-grade spelling bee would be going up against the top ten fifth-grade spellers. The winner of this spelling bee would be the top speller in our school and would go on to represent Pine Heights in the district spelling bee, and if they won that, in the county, and if that, the state, and if they won that, the country. And after that, the *world*.

If there was such a thing as a spelling bee for the world. Which, if there isn't, there totally should be.

And since I'd made the final ten of the fourth-graders, that meant I was going to be in this all-star finalist Pine Heights spelling bee.

You would think I would be happy about this, but of course I wasn't, because this was just going to be another opportunity for Rosemary to be all, "AL-LIE! AL-LIE!" and for me to fail and for her to knock me down and wipe me up like a mop. Of course I had already gotten Erica to promise she wouldn't let Caroline near any more of her mother's cookies, so Caroline wouldn't get sick this time. But still.

It was a good thing I had Grandma's visit (and getting to choose my kitten) to look forward to. Otherwise, I just might have given up entirely and gotten into bed and pulled the covers over my head.

But Grandma's visit was important to me, because I knew that finally I was going to have someone besides Dad to turn to for help with the Rosemary situation. Because Grandma was super old, and old people are good at giving advice about stuff (at least on TV). I figured if there was anybody who was going to be able to tell me what to do about Rosemary, it would be Grandma. I had once asked Grandma's advice about what to do about the fact that everywhere I went, people were always trying to serve me things with tomatoes in it. One of my main rules is, *Never eat anything red.*

But an important subrule of that is, *Never eat anything with tomatoes in it, or on it.* I hate tomatoes. And so, I was surprised to learn during Grandma's last visit, does Grandma!

So I figured if anyone knew how to handle the fact that everywhere you go, people are *always* offering you salsa or sandwiches with tomatoes on them, Grandma would.

So I asked her, and she said, "Just say no, thank you."

See? The woman is a genius. *Old people know everything.* That's a rule.

So by the time Friday rolled around, the day we were supposed to drive to the airport to pick up Grandma, I was looking forward to seeing her more than I could remember looking forward to practically anything (except finally getting Mewsette and being able to take her home and put her in her pink feathered canopy cat bed, when I finally get that, too).

And when we saw her coming down the escalator to the baggage claim area, I totally beat both Mark and Kevin rushing up to her and throwing my arms around her, even though I had to run up the down stairs a little to do it.

Grandma didn't mind, though. Even if maybe some of the other people getting off the escalator might have.

"Oh, Allie," she said, patting me on the head. "What an interesting hairstyle you've chosen."

"I did it myself," I told her. "It's three ponytails and a braid."

"I can see that," Grandma said. "Oh, hello, Mark and Kevin. Kevin, what is that you're wearing?"

"I'm a pirate, Grandma," Kevin said proudly.

"It's a phase, Ruth," Mom said, I guess seeing Grandma's confused look as she was going to kiss Grandma on the cheek. "How are you?"

"I'm well, thank you," Grandma said. "Don't you look shapely, Elizabeth. Hello, Thomas," she said to Dad. "And where is Jay?"

"Oh," Dad said, kissing Grandma on the cheek as well. "He had some important work to do. He'll join us at the restaurant for dinner, though."

"I'm sure he had some important work to do," Grandma said. "Undergraduate students who are in their sixth year of taking poetry classes always have very important work to do, indeed. What is it, Mark?" She looked down at Mark, who'd been tugging on her suit jacket.

"We made this for you," Mark said, holding up the sign. Mark had written WELCOME, GRANDMA in glue and sparkles on yellow construction paper. It was a pretty babyish sign, but Mark had decided he was never going to get his dirt bike if he didn't show some creativity.

"How lovely," Grandma said. "Why don't you hold on

117

to it for me?" You could tell Grandma didn't want to get sparkles on herself.

"Okay," Mark said, looking disappointed. It was as if he could practically see that dirt bike disintegrating before his eyes. I almost laughed at him, but then I remembered Mewsette's canopy cat bed. I seriously didn't want Mewsette to sleep in a tap-shoe box for the rest of her life.

"How was your flight, Grandma?" I asked.

"Horrible," Grandma replied as we all walked toward the baggage carousel her suitcase was supposed to come barfing out of. "How they think they can charge so much to jam so many people into such a small plane . . . and then they don't even serve you a meal!"

"We're going out for dinner tonight," Kevin volunteered. "Red Lobster! That's why I'm dressed like this. Pirates mostly ate seafood, you know, on account of they lived on the sea."

"You *always* dress like that," Mark pointed out to him. "And for your information, pirates ate mostly hardtack, which is a type of biscuit."

"Gosh," Kevin said, "I would know that if I had a book on pirates."

Mark and I gave Kevin disgusted looks, neither of us able to believe he'd gotten in his present request so fast. Especially since he was asking for a book, and he can't even read yet.

We needn't have worried, though, since Grandma wasn't even paying attention.

"I don't know if I want to go out tonight," she was saying. "I'm so exhausted from that horrible flight. I think I'd like a nice hot bath and maybe a grilled cheese sandwich before bed."

"Well," Dad said, "that isn't going to happen, unless we go out for grilled cheese sandwiches. Because we don't have a stove yet."

Grandma looked shocked. *"What?"* she said, staring at Dad.

"Ruth, we told you," Mom said. "Remember? Our oven hasn't been installed yet. It hasn't arrived from the distributor."

"But that's ridiculous," Grandma said. "You moved weeks ago. What have you been feeding these children?"

"Hot Pockets, mainly," I explained. "And microwaved oatmeal for breakfast."

"And popcorn," Mark said. "But just that one time."

"Oh, look," Mom said as the baggage carousel started to move. "Here comes the luggage. What does your suitcase look like, Ruth?"

"It's gray with a red ribbon on the handle," Grandma said. "Thomas, this is ridiculous. Why haven't you called the company you ordered the stove from and demanded they deliver it immediately?"

"Well," Dad said, "we tried that, Mother. But the model we want is on back order."

"Well, just pick a different kind," Grandma said.

"We don't want a different kind, Mother," Dad said. "We want that kind."

"Don't be simpleminded," Grandma said. "Ovens are all the same. Just get a different one."

"Ruth," Mom said, "our house is over a hundred years

120

old. We want an oven and stovetop that fit in with the character of our home."

"Is that your bag, Grandma?" Mark asked, pointing at a gray bag with a red ribbon around the handle.

"No," Grandma said. "But surely there is some other oven that would meet your requirements."

"There really isn't," Mom said. "The one we want has six burners, a built-in pancake griddle, and a warming rack for freshly baked bread."

"Is that your bag, Grandma?" Mark wanted to know, pointing at another gray bag with a red ribbon on the handle.

"No," Grandma said. "Why on earth would anyone need six burners? Are you planning on cooking for the U.S. Army, perhaps?"

"Grandma," I said, feeling desperate all of a sudden. I hadn't brought a welcome sign or worn a pirate costume. All I'd done was put my hair in a particularly attractive style. "Did you hear? I'm in a spelling bee! Not just any spelling bee, but against fifth-graders —"

"Is that it, Grandma?" Kevin wanted to know, practically throwing himself on another gray suitcase. "Is it?"

"Yes, that's it," Grandma said. "Somebody grab it before it goes around again!"

Mark threw himself on Grandma's bag, landing on the conveyor belt so that he started going around with the suitcases. This caused Kevin to scream in terror and Mom to start running after Mark, to the annoyance of all the people who were trying to get their bags.

"Dad," I yelled. "Do something!" I didn't want Mark to get sucked behind the big rubber flap at the end of the baggage carousel.

"Well, don't just stand there, Thomas," Grandma said, recognizing the danger of the big flap as well (although Mark would probably think it was cool to go through the big flap).

But, fortunately, Mom and Dad were both on it, Dad grabbing Mark and yanking him off the baggage carousel (and also halfway into the air), and Mom grabbing Grandma's suitcase, just as the two of them were about to go under the rubber flap.

"Well," Grandma said when Mom and Dad came back to where we were standing, both of them panting a little. "That was exciting."

Two hours later (because the airport is pretty far from where we live), we were all sitting around a table at Red Lobster. We kids were on our best behavior, because the last few times we'd been out to dinner, some pretty bad stuff had happened. We'd been asked never to dine at the Waffle House, the International House of Pancakes, and the Lung Chung Chinese Restaurant again due to the bad behavior of my little brothers and, occasionally, myself. Although in my own defense, my bad behavior was to protect an innocent turtle, who now lives with my uncle Jay.

But so far we'd never gotten kicked out of Red Lobster. Mom and Dad had told us if we did anything tonight to embarrass them with Grandma, they would personally take away our television privileges until we were in high school, plus we would never see dessert until the year 2042. In addition, I wouldn't get my kitten, Mark could kiss any chance of getting a dirt bike good-bye, and they'd take away Kevin's pirate costume.

This seemed unnecessarily harsh to me. I thought just telling me I'd never get a cell phone would be threat enough. I have only been dying for one since forever.

Grandma didn't really have much of a chance to check out the new house when we took her there before dinner to drop off her suitcase and let her "freshen up." The guest room where she was staying is in a different part of the house from where we kids sleep. Mom and Dad had given us a whole floor to ourselves, where it was just our three rooms and a bathroom (and the attic, which I used to think was haunted, but I don't anymore).

The guest room used to be the maid's room. Our house was so old it was built back in the days when people had maids and butlers who lived with them. But that doesn't mean our house is nice. Maybe it used to be, but over the years the people who have lived in it just basically let it fall apart until my parents bought it and decided to fix it up — something they are still doing, slowly. Mom was mostly done with the painting and wallpapering, but she still had a ways to go with some rooms.

Grandma's room was done, though, and it looked totally

pretty. Mom had painted the walls a really nice pinky beige —"blush" is what it said on the paint can — and put a pretty pink rug on the wood floor and hung lace curtains that matched the bedspread, and the bed had one of those wrought-iron frames and the room had its own closet and a little bathroom with a bathtub with a built-in shower.

When Mom asked Grandma if her room was all right, she said, "It will do," which made Mom's mouth shrivel up to the size of a penny. When we got to the restaurant, Mom ordered a Manhattan on the rocks, which is a drink she usually only gets on her birthday. So Mark asked if all of us kids could get Shirley Temples, which we normally aren't allowed to have except on *our* birthdays, because Mom says they are pure sugar. But tonight she said, "Sure, why not?"

We were enjoying our Shirley Temples and trying not to do anything bad — I wasn't, for instance, looking anywhere near the giant tank that held all the live lobsters, thinking about how mean it was of Red Lobster to let their customers pick out a lobster from that tank and then have the chefs kill it and serve it to them, especially since lobsters mate for life and can sometimes be seen holding claws with their lobster husband or wife on the bottom of the ocean — when Uncle Jay finally got to the restaurant with his girlfriend, Harmony, their cheeks looking all rosy from the cold outside.

"Ma," Uncle Jay said, unwinding his scarf and leaning down to give Grandma a kiss on the cheek. "Nice to see you. You look great, as always."

"Jay," Grandma said calmly as Uncle Jay sat down between me and Mark (we'd saved him a place) and Harmony sat down by Kevin.

"Ma, this is my girlfriend, Harmony Culpepper."

"How do you do, Mrs. Finkle?" Harmony said, holding out her hand across the table to shake Grandma's hand. "It's so nice to finally meet —"

But Grandma was staring at Uncle Jay. "Are you growing a *beard*?"

"It's a goatee," Uncle Jay said. "I'm just trying something new." He opened his menu as Harmony dropped her hand, realizing Grandma wasn't going to shake it. "So what are we having?"

"We're having Shirley Temples!" Kevin screamed, lifting up his eye patch so he could see Uncle Jay more clearly.

"Hitting the hard stuff already," Uncle Jay said. "I'm down with that. The lady and I'll have Cokes," he told the waitress. "And you better keep 'em coming. So how was your flight, Ma?"

Grandma told Uncle Jay all over again about how terrible the airlines were, while the rest of us read the menus and figured out what we wanted to eat. Red Lobster is one of Kevin's favorite restaurants because it's pretty fancy, and he likes everything fancy, and also it has a nautical theme, and he likes pirates. And Mark likes it, too, because just about his favorite thing to eat in the world is fish-and-chips.

But Red Lobster is probably my most hated restaurant in the whole world, because it violates my two biggest food rules — *Never eat anything red*, and *Never eat anything that once swam in the ocean.* I am not a vegetarian, although I tried to be for one day once until Dad took us to McDonald's and I couldn't resist the smell of the delicious burgers there.

I just don't like fish. I don't like how fish tastes. It tastes . . . well, like fish. Back when we had an oven, Mom tried to make fish every way there was to make it — fried, broiled, baked. Nothing. I didn't like it any way there is to prepare it. She even took me out for sushi once. No way. I just don't like fish. I don't like shrimp, I don't like lobster, I don't like scallops, I don't like tuna fish sandwiches, although I do like goldfish crackers. I just don't eat anything that once lived in the water.

This is a rule.

So when we go to Red Lobster, I order a hamburger. With no ketchup or tomato.

The fact that I don't like fish shouldn't bother anyone else. It really isn't anyone else's business. It doesn't hurt anyone but me, and maybe my parents, because on the nights that we are having something fishy, they have to make me something else, such as peanut butter and jelly (with grape, not strawberry, jelly).

But I don't mind. It's not a big deal. Except maybe when I am eating at someone else's house and they serve tuna salad sandwiches and I have to hide mine in my napkin and flush it down the toilet later.

But when the waitress came around to take our dinner orders and I asked for a hamburger, well done (because I don't like to see any red parts, on account of not eating anything red), Grandma went, "Don't be ridiculous, Allie. Why are you getting a burger? You're in a place that specializes in fish. Why don't you order the fish-and-chips, like Mark?"

"Allie doesn't like fish, Mother," Dad explained.

"Allie's a carnivore," Uncle Jay said, toasting me with his Coke. "Aren't you, Allie?"

"How's your kitten, Allie?" Harmony asked, smiling. Harmony has a beautiful smile. Plus, she's very nice.

"Well," Grandma said, "then why doesn't she get some shrimp, like Kevin?"

"Because she doesn't like shrimp, either, Ruth," Mom said, taking a sip from her drink, which had a fancy umbrella in it. "She's fine with just a burger."

"Yes, ma'am," I said, because Dad had told us in the car on the way to the airport never to say yeah to Grandma, but always yes, ma'am. "I'm fine with just a burger."

"That's ridiculous," Grandma said with a harumphing sound as she stared down at her menu. "Getting a burger at a fish place." Then, shaking her head, she ordered a lobster dish from the waitress.

Tears filled my eyes. I couldn't believe it! Not only had Grandma disapproved of me ordering something different from everybody else — when she, of all people, should know better (being a fellow tomato hater) — but she was killing one of the lobsters from the tank! How could I ask her advice regarding what to do about Rosemary now, when it was clear she didn't even care about the life of a possibly monogamous crustacean?

I was trying hard not to let my tears spill out and splash onto the tablecloth when I felt a warm hand settle over mine. I looked up and saw Uncle Jay smiling down at me from between the brown bristles of his mustache.

"Don't let her get to you, Allie," he whispered while Grandma was busy arguing with the waitress about how she wanted her lobster broiled and not steamed. "It's not worth it."

"I don't know what you're talking about," I said, looking away. I knew Uncle Jay and Grandma didn't get along. They haven't seen eye to eye ever since Uncle Jay dropped out of the premed program at the university and decided to study poetry instead. Grandma doesn't think there's any future in poetry. Which makes it clear she has never heard of the poem "Twinkle, Twinkle, Little Star."

"Yeah," Uncle Jay said, giving my hand a pat, "I think you do. But you're a tough kid. You'll work it out on your own. You always do."

I didn't know what he was talking about. I'm not a tough kid. If I was a tough kid, I wouldn't be so nervous about this spelling bee coming up. I'd have punched Rosemary in the nose already. I'd have told Grandma I had every right to order a burger in a fish place if I wanted to.

Instead, I just sat there, trying not to cry.

Which just went to show that Rosemary was right: I was a scaredy-cat, and not an alley cat, after all.

RULE #8

It's not Polite to Stare

Every day at lunchtime and recess when we weren't keeping an eye out for Rosemary, Erica and Sophie helped Caroline and me study for the champion spelling bee instead of playing queens. It was extra hard because in addition to studying the fourth-grade spelling bee list, we had to study the fifth-grade list, too, which included words like "giraffe" (easy — I mean, I not only knew how to spell "giraffe," I knew baby giraffes gestated between fourteen and fifteen months) and "pasteurize" (not so easy, but it *is* written on every milk carton we've been drinking from since, like, forever).

Sophie suggested that, since we'd formed our own study

group, we maybe let some of the other kids in the fourth-grade final ten in on it.

Caroline said, "Oh, that's a good idea. Lenny could use the practice," but Erica said, teasingly, "I think she means Prince Peter," which caused Sophie's whole head to turn the color of my hot pink leggings.

So then Erica apologized profusely, because that's what Erica always does when she's hurt someone's feelings, and even sometimes when she hasn't. Sophie tried to laugh it off, saying Prince Peter was so perfect he didn't need any practice, but we all knew she was embarrassed, so we politely let the subject drop and played a quick round of queens — with no mention of Prince Peter — to get our minds off the subject.

We were crawling out of the bushes that hid our special secret fortress from view when a terrible thing happened. Someone over on the baseball diamond kicked a foul ball and it rolled near us, and Rosemary Dawkins came running after it and saw us emerging from the twisted shrubs that guarded our refuge.

She picked up the ball and, ignoring the cries of "Kick it back!" and "Rosemary! Rosemary! Over here!" coming from behind her, studied us unsmilingly, with her eyes narrowed.

"So that's where you disappear to every day," she said to me. Not in a friendly voice. Not in a friendly voice at all.

I had straightened up, having finished crawling out from beneath the bushes, and now I was picking dead leaves from my hot pink leggings. I was standing too far away from Rosemary for her to hit me, unless she came at me very quickly. Still, I studied the distance between us. She would have to come at me uphill. This would put me at a distinct height advantage. I could easily reach her nose from where I was standing.

This thought was making my heart pound. I really did not want to fight Rosemary.

But I also really did not want to get knocked down and wiped up like a mop.

I made my hand into a fist, thumb on the outside, just to get ready.

"Rosemary," Caroline said. "Go away. We aren't bothering you."

"Y-yeah, Rosemary," Sophie said, her voice shaking a little. "I think the people you're playing with want the ball back."

Rosemary turned around to stare at — my brother Mark, of all people. He'd come running up.

"Rosemary," he said, completely ignoring me. *You have to ignore your siblings on the playground at school unless one of them is bleeding or otherwise in pain.* This is a rule. "Are you still playing? Can we have the ball back or what?"

Rosemary turned around and threw the ball at him. It bounced once on the gravel and would have spun up and hit Mark in the face if he hadn't caught it with a disgusted look, then turned around and raced back to the kick ball game.

So much for my brother finding out who the girl was who wanted to beat me up.

"What's back there?" Rosemary wanted to know, tilting her head at the bushes we'd just come crawling through.

"Nothing," I said quickly. I could see where this was going, and it was making me very, very afraid — more afraid, even, than the thought of Rosemary's fist in my face. I didn't want Rosemary finding out about our secret fortress and telling the whole class about it. It was *our* secret place! It didn't have anything to do with her! I didn't want to share it with anyone else! It belonged to Erica, Caroline, and Sophie, who'd been nice enough to share it with me, the New Girl.

And I wasn't about to let it get ruined just because Rosemary didn't like me.

"Let me see," Rosemary said, taking a step toward me, up the steep little hill from the playground toward the bushes.

"No," I said, taking a step toward her, down the hill. My heart was beating harder than ever. I felt so sick to my stomach, I thought I might throw up the microwaved oatmeal Dad had made me (over Grandma's strenuous objections. She said children should have a proper breakfast of eggs and bacon) that morning.

Still. I wasn't going to back down. I kept my fist at my side, ready to meet Rosemary's nose if the situation absolutely called for it and a nonviolent resolution to the conflict couldn't be found.

For a horrible, stomach-clenching, heart-pounding moment, I thought Rosemary was going to grab me and throw me to the ground or try to punch *me* in the nose.

But instead, to my incredible relief, the warning bell went off. Morning recess was over. It was time to get into our lines and go inside to class.

The only problem was, Rosemary didn't move.

So neither did I. We both just stood there, staring at each other. I wanted to look away — I wanted to *run* away. But I was afraid if I did, Rosemary might come after me and hit me, and I wouldn't see her fist coming.

"It's time to go back to class," Erica said, her voice sounding a little high-pitched and wobbly. "You guys? We have to go now."

"Fine," Rosemary said, still staring at me. "But this isn't over."

"Fine," I said, staring right back at her.

"Fine," Rosemary said. Then she let out a laugh and tossed her long, bushy hair, and said, *"Scaredy-cat."*

And then she turned around and ran as hard as she could for the line. And I stood there watching her go, feeling like Jell-O — like I had no bones at all in my body, just blood and skin and maybe a little muscle, but not any that could actually support my body. Erica put her arm around my shoulders and whispered, "It's okay. We wouldn't have let her hurt you."

And Caroline and Sophie said the same thing and patted me on the arms, and I totally believed them.

Except that, really, what could they have done to stop her?

It was a big relief when lunchtime rolled around that day. I couldn't wait to get home and have some microwaved hot dogs or some French bread pizza. Since Grandma was visiting, I thought maybe Mom might step it up and maybe even whip up some Hot Pockets. I really wasn't prepared for the scene that greeted us when Kevin and I stepped through the mudroom door, a few minutes behind Mark, who as usual had hitched a ride home on the back of one of the neighborhood boys' dirt bikes.

And that was Mom standing in the kitchen next to a brand-new stove, which some men from Home Depot were holding on a dolly, while Grandma stood nearby, looking like she was pretty angry. But not as angry as Mom, maybe.

"No, Ruth," Mom was saying. Well, she wasn't really saying it, exactly. She was sort of shouting it. "No, I guess you're right. I guess I don't appreciate the gesture. I already have a stove."

"Clearly," Grandma said, almost shouting, too, "you do not. That is why my grandchildren have been eating microwaved meals for the past few weeks. That's why I simply went to the store this morning and bought this perfectly nice stove and had it delivered without any problem, as you can see —"

"As we explained to you last night," Mom yelled, "the stove we ordered *from the same store you went to* is on back order. It's arriving at the end of the month. We already have a stove, Ruth. It's just not here."

"But what's wrong with this one?" Grandma wanted to know, pointing at the stove the men were holding on the dolly. "It's here. It's ready to be installed. The children can have grilled cheese for their lunch."

Mark, Kevin, and I exchanged glances. It had been a long time since we'd had grilled cheese. I personally love grilled cheese.

But even from where I was standing, I could see there was a lot wrong with the stove Grandma had picked out. It looked kind of modern and shiny, and even in the short time I had lived in our new house, I knew that wasn't the style Mom and Dad were going for. They wanted the things inside of it to match the old-fashionedness of the house. Shiny and modern didn't go with the rest of the kitchen, which was snug and comfy.

"It's just not the stove we ordered," Mom said, proving I was right. "And that we already paid for."

"I'm sure you can get your money back," Grandma said, glancing at the men who were holding up the stove. They looked like they were getting kind of tired of holding the stove. I'm sure it was heavy. "Can't she?"

"I don't know anything about that, ma'am," said the man holding the dolly in a bored voice. "We're just here to make the delivery. Do you want it or not?"

"Yes," Grandma said, at the same time that Mom said, "No!"

At that moment, fortunately, Dad came home from the department where he works. He walked in and said to Mom, "I got your message. What's the —"

Then he saw the stove, and the men from Home Depot, and Grandma. And he said, "Oh."

The men holding the stove seemed relieved to see Dad, like maybe they thought, finally, here was someone they could ask what was going on.

"Where can we put this?" they wanted to know.

"Back on the truck," Dad said. "That's not the oven we ordered."

"Thomas!" Grandma cried.

"Kids," Mom said. "Get in my car. We're going out for lunch."

"Yay!" Mark and Kevin screamed. "McDonald's!"

We almost never get to eat McDonald's, because Mom

considers it junk food, and we aren't supposed to have junk food. But sometimes, on special occasions — like now — one of my parents will break down and let us have a hamburger with a small order of fries and a milk — never a Coke. That day is always a good day.

But while we were feasting on this unexpected bounty, my day suddenly got a thousand times better, because Mom's cell phone rang, and it was Mrs. Hauser to find out when we could stop by to see Lady Serena Archibald's kittens, who had finally started to sprout some fur and open up their eyes.

"Well," Mom said, looking at her watch. "How about now?"

I nearly choked on a fry. "Now? But we have school. And what about Dad and Grandma? Don't you have to go home and see Dad and Grandma?"

"Now would be perfect," Mom told Mrs. Hauser.

The next thing I knew, we were standing on the Hausers' fancy front porch in the suburbs, ringing the doorbell, and Mom was telling Kevin and Mark that if they touched anything or embarrassed her in any way, she would make sure Grandma found out, and they could kiss any chance of getting their pirate book or dirt bike good-bye.

Then Mrs. Hauser was opening the door, looking very sophisticated (fifth-grade spelling word) in a beige silk pantsuit with little beige high heels with feathers on the toes. Mrs. Hauser always dressed up, even when she was just at home by herself like today. She also always wore a lot of perfume and makeup, including lip liner, which I saw Kevin staring at, even though *It's not polite to stare* (this is a rule).

She screamed with happiness when she saw my mom and leaned over and kissed the air next to Mom's face and said how happy she was to see her. Then she did the same thing to me. Then she told my brothers there were freshly baked chocolate chip cookies on a plate in the kitchen, and that they should go help themselves, and pointed to where the kitchen was.

This was all my brothers needed to hear. They ran off and we didn't see them for, like, half an hour.

"Now, Allie," Mrs. Hauser said. Mrs. Hauser knows I want to be a vet, and so she talks to me about her cat like

I'm a grown-up, which I appreciate. "You can't imagine how frightened I was these past few weeks. I mean, Lady Serena Archibald of course is an incredible kitty, as you know, but I had no idea whether or not she had any natural maternal instincts. But she's been remarkable, just remarkable. Of course I made a nursery for her in the den, but she would have none of it, just none of it, and wouldn't you know she carried every single one of those kittens upstairs in the middle of the night and put them in my closet right on top of my Manolos? Well, I always did know she had style — just not how much style! So that's where they are now, and I suppose that's where they intend on staying."

As she'd been speaking, Mrs. Hauser was leading me and Mom up a wide circular staircase to the second floor of her house and through the thick cream-colored carpeting to her bedroom, and then into her huge bedroom closet.

"Now, Lady Serena lets *me* near her babies, of course," Mrs. Hauser said as she pushed back a lot of dresses and skirts so we could see where Lady Serena was hiding with her kittens. "But I don't know how she'll feel about strangers. Not that you're a stranger, of course she loves you,

Allie, but she's very protective of her little boys and girls. Let's see how she's feeling today."

And then Mrs. Hauser sank down on her knees and indicated that I should do the same, so I did. And she started sorting through a lot of shoe boxes that were lying on the carpeted floor, and saying in a soft voice, "Here, puss, here, baby . . ."

And then, my heart thudding softly in anticipation, finally, I saw her . . . beautiful Lady Serena Archibald, with her long silky gray fur and her funny, smushed-in face, lying in a big box on top of a pair of suede boots, with six tiny squirming little bodies on top of her.

"Oh!" I cried. Because the little bodies didn't look like hairless pink newts at all but were all different colors, black, white, smoky gray like their mother, and one — yes, I could see one, peeping in and out as it crawled all over the place — that was gray with black smudges like stripes and white smudges on its feet like little socks.

"What's THAT one?" I wanted to know, pointing.

"What one, honey?" Mrs. Hauser asked. It was kind of hard to tell one kitten from the other because they were all scrambling over one another and making the faintest little mewing sounds. Over it all, you could hear Lady Serena Archibald purring like a vacuum cleaner. She didn't seem to mind us visiting her at all.

"The little one with the stripes," I said.

"Oh, isn't that one a little sweetheart?" Mrs. Hauser asked. "I know. Brittany calls that one Stripey."

I didn't want to hear about what Mrs. Hauser's daughter, Brittany, was calling MY kitten. Stripey was a totally unimaginative name for a striped cat, anyway.

"Is Stripey a boy kitten," I asked, "or a girl kitten? I really want a girl kitten."

"Well, let me see," Mrs. Hauser said. And she reached into the boot box and picked up the tiny kitten.

"Excuse me, Mama," she said to Lady Serena, who just purred harder. Then she tilted up the striped kitten and looked beneath its tail.

Please, I prayed. Let it be a girl. After my rotten, rotten day — my rotten year — let it be a girl.

"You're in luck," Mrs. Hauser said. "Stripey's a girl!"

I let out a weird, squeaking sound I was so happy and threw a look at my mom, sitting on the bed a few feet away. She smiled back at me.

"Can I hold her?" I asked Mrs. Hauser.

"Of course you can," Mrs. Hauser said, and passed the tiny kitten to me. "But be careful. Her eyes have only been open for a few days. Everything is very new to her."

"I will be," I said, and held out my hands for Mrs. Hauser to put Mewsette into them for the very first time.

I couldn't believe how little she was! Smaller than one of my hands! And she weighed practically nothing. She was light as a feather. And as soft as one, too. She had a white belly and throat, and a gray back and tail with black stripes, and white feet, and a pink nose and bright blue eyes that looked into mine with a wide-eyed, confused gaze, as if to say, "Are you my mom? Hey, no, you're not. Where's my mom?"

She was completely perfect in every way. I wanted to take her home right then and there, but I knew she wasn't ready, and neither was I. I didn't have her food or food bowls or litter box. I didn't have her pink rhinestone collar or her pink feathered canopy cat bed. I had a lot of stuff to do to get ready for her!

Looking at me looking down at her, Mewsette opened her mouth and went, "Aarh?"

Mrs. Hauser laughed. "She likes you!"

"I love her," I said simply. Because it was true.

"Are you sure?" Mom asked from the bed. "You haven't even looked at the other kittens."

"No," I said. I didn't need to look at the other kittens. "This is my kitten. This is Mewsette."

"Mewsette," Mrs. Hauser said. "What a pretty name. Much nicer than Stripey."

I didn't want to say "I know," because that would have been rude. Instead I just said, "Thank you." *The polite thing to say when someone gives you a compliment is Thank you.* That's a rule. It's rude to say anything else, really.

"Mewsette," I said to Mewsette, seeing how she liked her name. She went, "Aarh?" again, and Lady Serena answered back with a "Maowr?" and Mewsette started looking around for her mom, so I figured it was best to return her to the boot box.

So I did, and quick as a wink her brothers and sisters started stepping on her head, but she got in there and started stepping on their heads right back at them. It was clear that Mewsette was a fighter. After all, she'd been through a lot.

Just like me.

"Oh, I'm so glad you all could come," Mrs. Hauser said, smiling at us. "So is today parent-teacher conferences or something in your new school district? How come you don't have to be in school?"

"We're just taking a little vacation," Mom said. "My mother-in-law is visiting."

"Oh," Mrs. Hauser said, with a laugh. "In that case, I bet you could use a freshly baked chocolate chip cookie, too."

"You know what?" Mom said. "I really could."

So we joined Mark and Kevin downstairs (they hadn't managed to break anything while we were gone) and had milk and cookies. I was a little worried because I was missing science class. I wondered if maybe Rosemary would think I was missing science because of her. Like, that I was afraid to come back after what had happened on the playground.

Would anyone believe me if I told them the truth, that I'd gone home for lunch and my grandma had tried to buy my parents a stove they hadn't wanted, so my mom had taken us to McDonald's, then to pick out my new kitten? *I* almost couldn't believe it, it seemed so unreal. And it was happening to me.

The truth was, my life was crazy. And about to get crazier than even I could have imagined. I didn't have the slightest idea.

RULE #9

If Someone Wants to Beat You Up, Try Psyching Her Out

When we got home from school later that day (Mom made Mark and me go back to Pine Heights after our visit to Mrs. Hauser's, even though I begged to have the rest of the day off because I didn't want Rosemary to continue what she'd started on the playground . . . only fortunately she got in trouble for headbutting Stuart Maxwell during PE so she had to stay in at afternoon recess and write an essay about the importance of learning to love your neighbor, so I was safe), the new stove was gone. And so was Grandma.

The stove had been taken back to the store. Grandma, it turned out, was just at Uncle Jay's apartment. She'd be back after dinner, which she was having with Uncle Jay and

Harmony. Mom was celebrating not having Grandma around by taking a long, hot bubble bath. We weren't supposed to disturb her. Instead, Dad let us watch all the television we wanted so long as we kept the volume down. It was like Christmas, Easter, and our birthdays all rolled into one. I remembered how much I loved it when Grandma came to visit. I called Erica and asked if she wanted to come over, and she did (she hardly ever gets to watch what she wants on TV, being the youngest child in a family of five). We watched two hours of Disney Channel and one hour of Nick uninterrupted. It was heaven.

Then we had home-delivered pizza for dinner, with cinnamon sticks for dessert that you dip into this kind of frosting. Erica asked if she could stay over for dinner, and my parents said yes and so did hers. We ate so much of the frosting stuff that we both nearly threw up. I told her all about Mewsette, and we had a good time setting everything up in my room in preparation for Mewsette's arrival. I explained how small Mewsette was and that the primary challenge would be to keep her from falling through one of the squares of the heating grate in the floor (it could happen), so we cordoned off a special area of my room that was just for Mewsette, blocking it off with my Polly Pocket Polly-Tastic Jumbo Jet Playset (whatever, it's not like I play with it anymore) and what was left of my geode collection.

Then we set up her temporary bed in Missy's tap-shoe box and pretended one of my old Beanie Baby kittens from the post office was Mewsette so we could practice taking care of her.

But it wasn't the same, really, as having a live kitten. Maybe because it had a forty-one-cent stamp as decoration on its rear end.

Finally, Dad yelled up the stairs that he was going to go pick up Grandma and did any of us want to go with him.

I didn't want to go because I was having a nice time hanging out with Erica, but then Dad said it wasn't actually a question, so Erica had to go home.

So Mark and Kevin and I all piled into the car and Dad drove us over to Uncle Jay's apartment building while Mom stayed home to clean up the dinner dishes. When we got to where Uncle Jay lived, Uncle Jay was sitting in the living room watching his TV that's as big as a normal person's couch, and Grandma and Harmony were nowhere to be seen. Uncle Jay explained that was because Harmony had gone home, and Grandma was in Uncle Jay's bedroom because she'd decided she was going to stay in a hotel, because she was so mad about Mom and Dad sending the stove back. She was on the phone calling around to different hotels, trying to get the most competitive rate.

"Jay," Dad said, sounding mad, "I thought you were going to talk to her."

"I did," Uncle Jay said. "And now she's mad at me, too."

"Great," Dad said. "Kids, wait here. I'm going to go talk to your grandma."

Mark and Kevin went to look at Wang Ba, Uncle Jay's pet turtle, who lives in the tub of his spare bathroom. That left me alone with Uncle Jay.

"Uncle Jay," I said, watching as some cops on the TV show he was looking at tackled a perp and his shirt came off as they put handcuffs on him. "Has anyone ever wanted to beat you up?"

"Sure," Uncle Jay said, "lots of times. Especially the year I lived in Shanghai. Why? Does someone want to beat you up?"

"Yeah," I said. "This girl in my new class named Rosemary."

Uncle Jay whistled and lowered the volume on his TV a little. "What did you do to her?" he wanted to know.

"I didn't do anything to her," I said with a shrug. "I'm just the New Girl."

"That'll do it sometimes, I guess," Uncle Jay said. "So, when's the fight going to go down?"

"I don't know," I said. "She just keeps saying she's going to kill me."

"She bigger than you?" Uncle Jay asked.

"Way bigger," I said miserably. "She's the biggest person in my class."

"Figures," Uncle Jay said. "You tell your mom and dad?"

"I told my dad," I said. "You know I can't tell my mom."

"Right," Uncle Jay said, nodding. He knew about the Kissing Kid, because I'd told him a long time ago. "Well, what did your dad say?"

"He showed me how to punch someone in the nose."

Uncle Jay looked impressed. "Really? Show me."

I showed him.

"Okay," Uncle Jay said. "You got a decent swing on you. Tell you what you do next. You gotta psych her out."

"Psych her out?"

"Right. I know what I'm talking about, because I'm a psych minor. And ninety-nine times out of a hundred with these bullies, they're bluffing. They don't really want to fight you."

I thought about Rosemary's face today on the playground.

"I don't think Rosemary's bluffing," I said.

"Well, you gotta find out," Uncle Jay said. "That's why next time she tells you she's going to kill you, you turn it

156

around. Tell her, 'No, actually, Rosemary, *I'm* going to kill *you*.'"

I love my uncle Jay. He's funny, and he saved Wang Ba when no one else would. Also, he always gives us whole cans of soda when we come over, and we aren't even allowed to have sugared soda at all. And he lets us watch whatever we want on his ginormous TV.

But he doesn't always give us the best advice.

"But I don't want to kill Rosemary," I said. "I just want to be friends with Rosemary."

"I know," Uncle Jay said. "That's the thing. She doesn't really want to kill you. And you don't really want to kill her. You're calling her bluff. When you say, 'Actually, Rosemary, *I'm* going to kill *you*,' she'll be so surprised, she'll back off."

"Actually," I said, "I think what she'll probably do is punch me in the face."

"No, she won't," Uncle Jay said. "But if she does, just punch her back."

"Okay, Uncle Jay," I said. "Thanks a lot for that advice."

This was basically the worst advice I had ever gotten from anyone. But *It's not polite to tell someone their advice stinks.* This is a rule. Especially since Uncle Jay has always been so nice to me.

So I just thanked him and kept watching TV with him. I didn't really know what else to do. Mark and Kevin came out a few minutes later and joined us, and we had a good time watching the cops on the TV show tell a lady who was yelling at them that her son had violated his parole and was going to jail whether she liked it or not. Which she didn't. She said a whole bunch of things about it, but you couldn't tell what they were because they all got bleeped out. Uncle Jay told us that this was an example of Americana at its finest, and that he was watching this show for his popular media class. Which meant he was taking a class where the homework was watching TV, which made me think I couldn't wait to get to college.

It was right after this that Dad came out with Grandma. Grandma didn't look too happy. Dad said, "Okay, I think we got that all straightened out. Grandma is going to come home with us now. Kids, you're happy Grandma is coming with us, aren't you? Because she has the craziest idea none of us care about her."

"I care!" Kevin yelled, jumping up from Uncle Jay's futon couch. "I care about you, Grandma!" Then he ran over and gave Grandma a hug. Mark and I exchanged glances because this was the fakiest display of affection either of us had ever seen, and we both knew it all had to do with a certain pirate book.

Then we remembered about the stuff we wanted Grandma to buy us. So we each popped up and ran over to give Grandma a hug, too.

It's not that I don't care about Grandma. I do. When she isn't saying mean things about what I've ordered in restaurants, Grandma is kind of cool. She has really pretty rings and she always smells good and she tells funny stories about Dad and Uncle Jay when they were little. When she isn't mad about something, Grandma is fun to have around.

The problem is, Grandma is usually mad about something.

Still, it wasn't her fault about the stove. She was just trying to be nice.

"Well," Grandma said, hugging us kids back — but just a little. "If you're all sure."

"They're sure, Ma," Uncle Jay said, not looking away from the TV.

"I don't know what Elizabeth is going to say," Grandma said.

"Mom wants you to come back, too, Grandma," Mark said, giving Grandma's legs an extra tight squeeze.

"Well, I suppose," Grandma said. "It's just till the end of the week, after all."

"You have to stay longer than that, Grandma," I said. "You have to stay long enough to see my new kitten!"

Mark shot me a mean look and hugged Grandma's legs tighter.

"No," he said. "You have to stay until Christmas!"

"No," Kevin said. "Until forever!"

"Let's not push it," Dad said. "Okay, come on, kids. Let's go home."

If Mom wasn't happy to see Grandma, she did a good job of pretending otherwise. She made a big fuss out of how glad she was that we were home and asking how Grandma's time with Uncle Jay had been (according to Grandma, not good: "How can he live like that? Like some kind of gypsy! If he'd stayed in the premed program, he'd have been in graduate school by now, and at the very least own his own home") and what she'd thought of Harmony (Grandma had liked her: "At least *she's* got some ambition").

Everything was going really well until bedtime, when Mom said, all casually, "Everyone better get plenty of sleep tonight, we have a big day tomorrow," and I was, like, "Why? What's tomorrow?" and Mom said, "Your big spelling bee, of course," and I was, like, "HOW DID YOU FIND OUT ABOUT THAT?" and Mom said Mrs. Harrington, Erica's mom, had told her. Also that Mom and Dad and Grandma and maybe even Uncle Jay and Harmony would be coming. COMING. To my spelling bee! In the middle of the day!

I told Mom that that really wouldn't be necessary. Also that she didn't understand. Pine Heights Elementary wasn't like my old school. Parents didn't come to things like the championship spelling bee between the fourth- and fifth-graders.

Also that if she came, it would totally embarrass me.

But nothing I said made any difference. Mom said she and Dad were completely proud of me for making it into the top ten spellers out of both fourth grades in the whole school, especially since spelling wasn't even one of my best subjects. They were both totally coming to the spelling bee, and there was nothing I could do about it.

This made me want to die. I went to bed unable to think of anything but how embarrassing it was going to be when all the fourth- and fifth-graders looked out and saw my parents — and *Grandma* — sitting in the gym. Why were they doing this to me? It wasn't fair. Why did I have to have the weirdest family in our whole town? Finkles weren't even funny. They were just plain STRANGE.

And tomorrow, everyone in my whole class was going to know it.

Including Rosemary.

Who would probably punch me in the face because of it.

RULE #10

If You Say It Enough Times in Your Head, It Will Come True (Sometimes)

"What I'm going to do," I explained to Erica on the way to school the next morning, "is just miss the very first word Mrs. Danielson gives me, and then I'll be out, and my family will go home, and that will be the end of it."

"But that's cheating," Erica said.

"It's not cheating if you get the word wrong on purpose," I said. "It's only cheating if you have the word written down somewhere and you peek at it and get it right."

Erica said, "I'm pretty sure if you spell it wrong on purpose, it's cheating."

"I don't care," I said. "I just want to sit back down."

"Well, don't tell Caroline," Erica said. "She doesn't like it when girls pretend to be dumb on purpose."

"Even when it's an emergency?" I asked in surprise. "Like, when the meanest girl in your class is going to kill you if you mess up, or if your family is going to embarrass you in front of the whole fourth grade?"

"And the fifth grade, too," Erica said just as we saw Sophie and Caroline crossing the street to join us.

"Don't mention anything to them about what we were just saying," I told Kevin, who was walking between us, holding both our hands, in a warning voice.

"I don't understand anything that's going on, anyway," Kevin grumbled. "No one ever tells me anything."

Sophie and Caroline couldn't stop talking about the spelling bee, Sophie because she was going to have a chance to gaze at Prince Peter all morning and Caroline because she was going to have another chance at being the best speller in our grade. Which was fine for them. Neither of them had parents who were insisting on showing up and mortifying them in front of the entire school.

Or a bully who was going to kill them if they messed up again.

But I'd learned my lesson. This time, I wasn't going to get myself into a situation where the gymnasium roof was going to reverberate with the sound of "AL-LIE! AL-LIE!" coming from Rosemary's direction. No way. I was going to quit while I was ahead. I wasn't, in fact, even going to try. I know what people say about how quitters never win and all of that.

But those people have never had Rosemary Dawkins threatening to put a fist in their guts. In this situation, quitting was the perfect solution!

But I took Erica's advice and didn't mention this to Caroline or Sophie. Or anyone at all. I sat at my desk and tried not to think about the spelling bee. During math, when Mrs. Hunter asked how many dogs there were at the ice rink if there were thirty legs on the ice including those belonging to seven humans, I correctly answered four (I always get the animal questions right. And most of the people and money ones right, too).

This made me feel good, and so did the note Erica passed me, a little drawing she'd made of Mewsette in her new sparkly collar (that I actually hadn't gotten yet).

But then I thought, what if I didn't get it? What if Grandma didn't like me anymore because I hadn't ordered fish at the restaurant, and I had to save up and buy Mewsette's collar myself? I had eleven dollars in my koala head purse. But that's only enough for the collar, not the cat bed. I'd have to ask for the bed for Christmas. But Christmas was *ages* away. Mewsette was going to have to sleep in the tap-shoe box, which really wasn't a proper box for such a beautiful kitten. At least, Mewsette would be a beautiful kitten when her fur started growing in. Right now she was a little ratty-looking. But that was because she was only a couple of weeks old, and she'd been born prematurely! Premature babies, even kittens, can't help how they look.

It was while I was worrying about all this — like I didn't have enough to worry about — that there was a knock on the classroom door and Mrs. Hunter called, "Come in," and Prince Peter opened the door and stuck his head in and said, "Mrs. Hunter, Mrs. Danielson says it's time," and my heart started slamming inside my chest, and Mrs. Hunter said, "Well, class, let's go."

So we all got up and got into our lines and filed downstairs to the gym. The whole time I was saying in my head, *Please don't let my parents and Grandma be there. Please don't let my parents and Grandma be there.* Because *If you say it enough times in your head, it will come true (sometimes).* That's a rule.

But not this time. Because when we walked into the gym, Mom and Dad and Grandma were sitting there in the last row, in the folding chairs Mr. Elkhart had put out for us kids to sit in. They were the only grown-ups in the room (besides teachers)! It was totally embarrassing.

As if that weren't awful enough, they *waved* at me as I went up to take my seat at the front of the room with the other championship spellers. Yes, that's right. They waved — and called, "Uncle Jay had class and couldn't make it!"— as I walked by.

To make matters worse, Erica, who is the world's friendliest person, totally waved back, and was, like, "Hi, Mr. and Mrs. Finkle!" even though I was doing my best to ignore them. Like, I wasn't waving back or anything. Erica grabbed the back of my hoodie and tugged on it and went, "Hey, Allie, your parents are here. Did you not see them? They're waving at you." Just in case the whole class hadn't noticed that my parents had come to the spelling bee.

Sophie and Caroline smiled and waved at my parents, too.

"That's so sweet of your mom and dad," Sophie said, and Caroline said, "You must be proud to have such supportive parents, Allie."

Oh, I was proud, all right. So proud I was hoping a meteor might hit the school and blow up just me.

When Rosemary saw what was going on — that the three adults in the gym who weren't teachers were parents and a grandma — worse, *my* parents and grandma — she got an evil look on her face. Just like I'd known she would. Then she started to laugh.

"Her parents came!" Rosemary gasped. She could barely speak, she was laughing so hard. "Her g-grandma came! T-to the sp-spelling bee! Oh, it's too funny! Somebody pinch me! I think I'm dreaming!"

One of the boys from the back row where Rosemary sits — Stuart Maxwell, I think — obliged Rosemary by pinching her, but I guess he did it too hard, because she said, "Ow!" and turned around and pinched him back even harder, making him squeal with pain.

"Class!" Mrs. Hunter gave us all the evil eye. It was amazing how such a pretty and stylish lady could look so scary when she wanted to. "Take your seats, please, and silently!"

We took our seats. I took mine at the front of the room, beside Caroline. The other champion spellers weren't being very silent, though. They were buzzing with excitement. Especially the fifth-grade girls, some of whom I recognized as being the same girls who'd thought Kevin was so cute that first day of school. They looked at me and whispered, "Oh, my gosh, it's her! The sister of the pirate!" and "It's the New Girl!" and "The New Girl's parents came to watch her in the spelling bee! Isn't that the cutest thing you've ever seen?" and "I could die! Look at her grandma! She's wearing a bun in her hair! She's so adorable! Like a grandma on TV."

I couldn't remember ever being so embarrassed in my life. I tried to think back, but I was pretty sure this was it. The time Mark dropped his plateful of Belgian waffles in front of the whole restaurant at the Easter buffet? Nope, this was more embarrassing. The time I begged and begged to be allowed to ride the pony at the horse park outside of Chicago when we went to visit Dad's friend, and then I fell off on my head? Totally more embarrassing than that. That other time I went down the Zoom Floom waterslide and I popped up out of the water at the end and my bikini top was gone? This was even more embarrassing.

"Caroline," I whispered.

"Yes," Caroline whispered back.

"Could you kill me now?"

"What? Why?"

"Because I'm so embarrassed."

"Why are you embarrassed?"

"Because my parents are here," I whispered. "With my grandma. They're the only parents who came out of the whole school."

"I think it's sweet," Caroline whispered back. "Besides, you didn't know any better than to tell them not to come. You're the New Girl. Remember?"

I wanted to tell Caroline that I had told my parents not to come — also, that I was tired of being the New Girl. How long was I going to have to be the New Girl, anyway? Before I had the chance, though, the spelling bee started. And the bad thing was, I sort of got so caught up in watching the fifth-grade girls who thought I was so cute miss *very easy* words like "calendar" and "scissors" that when Mrs. Danielson got to me I forgot to misspell my word ("tongue") and the next thing I knew Rosemary and the rest of Mrs. Hunter's class were chanting, "AL-LIE, AL-LIE," when it came to be my turn again!

It was just like last time! And I hadn't wanted it to get to this! I hadn't wanted there to be all this pressure!

I looked out into the gym and saw my parents sitting there with Grandma, looking just what Caroline had said — proud. Proud of me! Proud that I was the New Girl but so many kids knew my name (even though the main person chanting it hated me and wanted to kill me. They didn't know that part of it).

And I knew I couldn't miss my next word (at least, not on purpose). Because they'd be so disappointed in me! Even the fifth-grade girls were chanting it. You could hear my name all the way up to the steel rafters of the gym. *AL-LIE! AL-LIE!*

"Allie," Mrs. Danielson said. "Your word is 'squirrel.' 'Squirrel.'"

"Squirrel?" Were they kidding me? Could they give me easier words? Didn't they know I had been reading about the life cycle of the squirrel since the first grade? The squirrel is a small or medium-size rodent of the family Sciuridae. When squirrels are born, they're as pink and hairless as Mewsette was when she was born. Only baby squirrels are much smaller than kittens, of course.

"Squirrel," I said. "S-Q-U-I-R-R-E-L. Squirrel."

"That is correct," Mrs. Danielson said.

Everyone cheered, including Rosemary. My parents looked pleased. Even Grandma smiled. I was beginning to get excited. A lot of the fourth-graders had been knocked out. It was just me, Caroline, and Peter. The rest were all fifth-graders. Maybe I'd make it all the way to the end. I didn't think I'd be the champion speller of the school, but maybe I'd do so well I'd impress Rosemary, and she'd decide to declare a truce, and I wouldn't have to try to psych her out or punch her in the nose. Maybe I wouldn't have to spend every recess looking over my shoulder to see if she was following me, or checking to see if it was safe to come out of our secret hiding spot. Maybe I'd finally be able to fit in with her and not be the New Girl anymore.

But when two more fifth-graders got knocked out, and it was down to just me, Caroline, Peter, and two fifth-graders, and Mrs. Danielson called my name and said, "Allie, your word is 'warrant.' 'Warrant,'" I knew my dream of finally being friends with Rosemary had been just that. A dream.

Because "warrant"? I didn't even know what that was. That wasn't one of the words Sophie and Caroline and Erica and I had studied. That had to be a fifth-grade word.

"Could you use that in a sentence, please?" I asked.

"Certainly," Mrs. Danielson said. "The sheriff issued a warrant for Robin Hood's arrest."

That didn't help me at all! All I knew about the word "warrant" was that it sounded like warren, which I knew from my extensive animal reading was what rabbits lived in. At least I knew how to spell "warren."

"AL-LIE," Rosemary and everyone else chanted. "AL-LIE!"

It wasn't at all hard to think with all this going on. Not. Which Mrs. Hunter must have known, since she said, "Shhhh!"

When it quieted down, I said, "Warrant. W-A-R-R-E-N-T. Warrant."

"That is incorrect," Mrs. Danielson said. "You may go sit down with the rest of your class, Allie."

Oh, no! I'd gotten it wrong!

My cheeks burning red, I went to sit down by Erica and Sophie, who slid over to make room for me. I couldn't even look at my parents and Grandma, though I'm sure *they* were looking at *me*.

"You did so good!" Erica whispered, patting me on the back, just as Sophie whispered, "'Warrant' is a stupid word! That word wasn't even on the list! It must have been a fifth-grade word."

"Shhh," I said. I pretended like I didn't want us to get in trouble for chitchatting. But really, I was mortified about having missed such an easy word (Prince Peter had stood up and spelled it correctly right after me). How could I have been so dumb? And in front of Rosemary! She really was going to kill me now.

And Mom and Dad had seen me miss it, too. And Grandma. Like she didn't hate me enough already. Could things get any worse?

The spelling bee came to a pretty quick end after that. The words got harder and harder. You could tell the fifth-grade spelling list got abandoned in favor of the sixth-grade list, and then the seventh-grade list. Finally, after words like "bikini" and "graffiti" got tossed around, there was only one speller standing: Caroline Wu.

Afterward everyone gathered around Caroline to congratulate her, including my mom and dad and grandma.

"You did so well," Mom said to Caroline. "It's such a shame your father couldn't make it! We'll be sure to let him know what a great job you did."

"Uh," Caroline said as Mom pumped her hand up and down. You could tell what Caroline was thinking: *Parents don't come to the Pine Heights Elementary School spelling bees.* But she was too polite to say so. "Thanks, Mrs. Finkle!"

I knew what Erica was thinking as she looked at me and smiled. *Finkles are funny!* She was too nice to say it out loud, though.

"Mr. and Mrs. Finkle," Mrs. Hunter said, coming up to my parents. "How lovely of you to stop by and support your daughter. And is this Allie's grandmother?"

"Yes," Dad said, introducing Grandma to Mrs. Hunter.

"So nice to meet you," Mrs. Hunter said, shaking Grandma's hand. "Your granddaughter is a joy to have in the classroom."

I froze when I heard that. I was? I was a joy in the classroom? Really? A joy? What did I do that was such a joy? I chitchatted with my neighbor all the time. That wasn't particularly joyful, I knew that.

But I did raise my hand to answer all the time in math. And I always volunteered to take notes to Mrs. Jenkins. And I was one of the best spellers in the class (which was strange, because I hadn't been at my old school). And I drew excellent dogs.

"I think she's a joy as well," I heard Grandma telling Mrs. Hunter. "We're very proud of her."

I couldn't believe my ears. *Grandma* was proud of me? I thought she was disappointed in me for my refusal to eat anything that had once lived in the ocean.

When she saw me standing there, Grandma let go of Mrs. Hunter's hand and leaned down and gave me a hug.

"You were great!" she said.

"I was?" I couldn't hide my surprise. "But . . . I misspelled 'warrant.'"

"Oh, warrant," Grandma said, straightening up. "Who needs warrant? You were close enough. I'm really proud of you. You're one of the best spellers in your whole class — in your whole school!"

"Well," I said modestly, "that's true. And the best speller in school is one of my best friends."

"I want to buy you a special present today after school," Grandma went on, "to celebrate how well you did. I'll take you to the mall and buy you whatever you want. How would you like that?"

This was exactly what I'd been hoping to hear since Grandma got off her airplane, but what I'd been so sure was never going to happen because of the fish incident. Now that it was really happening, I couldn't believe it.

"Oh, Ruth," Mom said. "That isn't necessary. You don't have to buy the children things —"

"I'd love it!" I cried, interrupting Mom. "There's a cat bed I've been really wanting for Mewsette, it only costs forty-nine ninety-nine, and a pink rhinestone collar, it's only five ninety-five —"

"It would be my pleasure," Grandma said a little stiffly, looking right at Mom. "Since your parents wouldn't let me buy anything for the house."

"Mother," Dad said, but I didn't hear anything he might have said after that, because Sophie came over and grabbed my arm and started dragging me away, going, "Oh, my gosh, didn't Prince Peter look good in his brown sweater today? And when he came over and congratulated Caroline, wasn't that the most princely thing you've ever seen? I could have *died*, it was such a nice thing to do, and so like him, don't you think? You can tell he really respects intelligent women. I'm going to start studying really hard every night instead of watching *Hannah Montana*, I think."

"That's probably a good idea," I said.

But I wasn't really listening. Because I was watching Rosemary, who was goofing around with some of the boys from the back row of our class by grabbing them around the neck and then trying to shove their heads into the backs of some of the folding chairs. Mrs. Hunter was still talking to my parents so she hadn't noticed, which was unusual because normally she has eyes in the back of her head. The boys, being so much smaller than Rosemary, really couldn't fight her, and so a lot of them were ending up with their heads stuck into the folding chairs. She had wedged Joey Fields in there up to his armpits, and it looked like a pretty tight fit. He was kind of waving his arms, trying to get himself free, like a beetle that had fallen over onto its back and couldn't quite turn itself upright.

I saw Mr. Elkhart, the custodial arts manager, standing over in one corner of the gym waiting to put the folding chairs away and take out the the tables for lunch, watching the whole scene with a sad look on his face.

I knew how he felt. Rosemary made me feel sad, too.

But not because I wanted to put those folding chairs away and now I had to wait for those boys to figure out how to get themselves unstuck from them.

But because I knew that, one day, Rosemary was going to shove me inside one of them, too.

RULE #11

A Lady Never Raises Her Fist to Another

Grandma took me shopping at the mall that very afternoon. I wanted to go straight to the pet shop to show her the pink feathered canopy cat bed and collar I wanted to buy for Mewsette.

But Grandma wanted to stop and have a snack first. She called it "tea."

It wasn't really tea, though. Because neither of us was having tea. I was having an ice-cream sundae, and Grandma was having coffee. But she said it was still tea because it was teatime.

"So," Grandma said, putting artificial sweetener in her coffee, "tell me about your new school. It's a bit . . . shabbier than your old school, wouldn't you say?"

"Yes," I said. "The gym is also the auditorium and the cafeteria."

"I saw that," Grandma said. "Quite unsanitary, in my opinion. Do you like it?"

"I do," I said, surprising myself a little. I hadn't really thought about it. "I like my friends, and I like my teacher, Mrs. Hunter. She's so pretty. There's just . . ." I paused, realizing I'd been about to say, *There's just one girl I don't like, Rosemary,* before remembering I couldn't say anything to Grandma about Rosemary, because she'd be bound to tell Mom, who'd tell Mrs. Hunter, who'd say something to Rosemary, who'd pound my face in.

"There's just what?" Grandma asked.

"Nothing," I said quickly, taking a big bite of ice cream so my mouth would be too full to say anything more.

Grandma eyed me over her cup of coffee.

"Allie," she said, sweetly, "whatever it is, you can tell me. Remember, I raised two boys . . . including your uncle Jay. I've heard it all."

"Well," I said, after I'd finally swallowed the ice cream, "do you promise you won't tell Mom?"

"I think I can safely say," Grandma said, "your mother and I are not on very intimate terms at the moment."

I wasn't particularly sure what she meant by that, but it sounded like a promise to me.

"Well," I said, "there's this one girl, Rosemary. She totally hates me for some reason and says she's going to beat me up. I don't really know what to do about it. Dad says I should punch her in the nose —"

Grandma put her coffee cup down with a clink.

"You will do no such thing," she said. "Allie Finkle! What can you be thinking! A lady never raises her fist to another!"

"Really?" I looked guiltily at her. "But then what am I supposed to do about her? I don't want her to stuff my head in a chair."

"You will tell your mother about her," Grandma said. "And if you don't, I will."

"You just promised you wouldn't!" I cried. "And if you tell Mom, and Mom tells my teacher, and my teacher says something to Rosemary, or to Rosemary's parents, Rosemary'll just get more mad, and she'll make my life even more miserable than it is already. Believe me, it's happened to me before."

Grandma made her lips all small, which was funny, because Mom does that, too, when she's mad.

"Very well," Grandma said. "I won't say anything. But I don't approve. What can your father be thinking?"

Probably that he wished someone had taught him how to punch so he wouldn't have gotten the crud beaten out of him when he was my age, I thought.

But I didn't say that out loud.

Instead, I said, "Want to go pick out my present now?"

Grandma sighed and said, "All right."

But when she saw what it was I wanted, she asked, "Are you sure this is what you want?"

"Yes," I said, wondering what she meant. What else would I want? Couldn't she see how fabulous the collar was? It was pink. And it had *sparkles*.

"Wouldn't you rather have a pretty dress?" Grandma asked. "I saw some lovely ones when I was in the mall the other day."

A dress? What did I want with a dress? I could get a boring old dress *anytime*. I couldn't get a hot pink cat bed with a velveteen cushion and a feathered canopy anytime.

"Or a new doll?" Grandma looked hopeful. "What about a lovely new Madame Alexander doll? I could get you Jo from *Little Women*. You haven't read *Little Women* yet, but I can assure you that you'll love Jo, she's just like you. She wants to get into fights, too."

I could see that Grandma didn't understand me at all. I don't want to get into fights. I want to *avoid* fights. Only no one seems to be able to help me figure out how to do that.

"No," I said, showing her the cat bed. "This is what I want. This is what I really, really want."

Grandma sighed and said, "All right. If you're sure."

"I'm sure," I said, my heart leaping. The cat bed! Mewsette's cat bed! And pink rhinestone collar! My kitten was going to be the most stylish, most comfortable cat in the world!

On our way to the counter, I also saw a pretty silver water dish and food bowl, and since they were only four dollars each, Grandma agreed to buy me those, too. So now I had everything my kitten needed (except food, a litter box, litter, and her shots)! I was so happy with my present, I hugged it to my chest the whole way home (well, as much as you could hug an enormous canopy cat bed).

It was when we walked in the door that Mom delivered the bad news. Or the good news, depending on the way you looked at it.

"Mrs. Hauser called," she said. "Lady Serena Archibald has developed an infection."

"Yeah," Dad said. "Mrs. Hauser finally decided she wants her Manolo Blahnik boots back."

Mom turned around and gave Dad a dirty look before she went on.

"Lady Serena's going to be all right, but she can't nurse anymore. All her kittens are being fostered out to people the vet's office has found, but Mrs. Hauser thought since you already picked the striped one, you might like to take her early —"

I gasped. Bring Mewsette home now? Tonight?

"But before you say anything," Mom went on, "I told her it's too much responsibility for a nine-year-old. A kitten that was already premature and isn't even weaned is too young —"

"No, it's not!" I yelled. "I can do it!"

"Allie," Mom said, looking desperate. "That kitten has to be given a special formula, and it will have to be fed with a sterilized bottle every few hours. What about when you're in school?"

"Well," Grandma said, putting down her purse, "I can do it, while I'm here."

Dad looked at Grandma in surprise. "Mother. Are you sure?"

"Really, Ruth," Mom said. "That's very nice, but —"

"It's just a kitten, Elizabeth," Grandma said. "Honestly. How much responsibility can it be?"

"Yeah," I said, feeling a huge burst of love for Grandma. I took back every mean thought I'd just had about her. "And I'm going to be a vet someday, Mom. I've read every book in the library on the care and feeding of cats. I know exactly what to do. I know I'll have to take care of her the way Lady Serena Archibald would have. I won't go to any sleepovers or to the mall or anything. That's okay. I'll feed her before school and when I come home for lunch and as soon as I get home from school and before dinner and before bed, and in the middle of the night, and I'll get Erica to come here and help me take care of her, and Sophie and Caroline will want to help, too —"

"I want to help," Mark said, coming into the kitchen from the TV room. He didn't look like he was joking, either.

"Me, too," Kevin said, following him. "I want to help with Mewsie."

Mom looked at all of us. Then she looked at Dad.

"Well," he said with a shrug, "it *is* just a kitten, after all, Liz."

Then Mom looked at the ceiling. Then she took a deep breath.

Then she let go of it.

"All right," she said. "We can try it."

We all started screaming. Well, me, Mark, and Kevin, which caused Marvin, who was lying on the kitchen floor, to start barking.

Mom had to shout the next part to be heard above the yelling: "But if it gets to be too much, we're giving her to one of the foster people the vet found."

Which was how, five hours later, I was lying in my sleeping bag inside the barrier I had made in my room, which wasn't so much to keep Mewsette in as to keep Marvin out, in case he wandered into my room — not that I thought he'd do anything to Mewsette, but he might have germs on him that wouldn't be good for such a little kitten until she got a bit older — looking at the tiny kitten Mom and I had picked up, along with the kitten nursing kit Mrs. Hauser had given us. I couldn't believe I had her at last — and that she was mine! It was like a dream come true.

I had put Mom's heating pad under the tap-shoe box so the heat wouldn't be too much — just enough, and hopefully just like what she was used to. I'd wanted to tuck Mewsette into her pink feathered canopy cat bed, but Mrs.

Hauser said the people at the vet's office had recommended a small box for now, saying it would make a tiny kitten feel more secure.

And I wanted Mewsette to feel very secure. I was hoping she wasn't missing her brothers and sisters and mom too much. I felt so bad for her! Her first night away from home! I remembered what it was like the first time I came to this house, how creepy and new it had felt. I hoped she didn't feel that way. She certainly seemed to have liked the food I'd made her. It hadn't looked too good to me — a powdered mix that came from the vet's office and you added water to — but Mewsette had gobbled it down like it was ice cream, maybe because she hadn't gotten too much food back home at the Hausers' because of having to fight all those other kittens for it, and then Lady Serena getting sick and all.

The amazing thing was, as much as she'd eaten already, she'd be hungry again in a few hours. I knew I'd be tired — it would be the middle of the night when she woke up again for her next feeding — but that was okay. When it's your kitten, you don't mind being tired. Besides, she'd be ready to eat regular kitten food in a few weeks, and by that time we'd be the best friends in the whole world.

Grandma had promised to look after her when I was at school, and Mom and Dad had said they would, too. Even Uncle Jay had said he would stop by between classes after Grandma went back home and help out with what he was calling Operation Mewsette.

"Animal Activist Allie, at Work Again," he said when he came over for dinner (Indian food delivery) that night. "Did you know veterinarians have to go to college for eight years?"

"So?" I'd asked, gnawing on some naan, which is Indian bread and is very good.

"You really want to go to college for eight years just so you can stick your hand up some horse's behind?"

"I imagine veterinarians get paid a good deal more than poets these days," Grandma observed.

"Touché," Uncle Jay said, and helped himself to more tandoori chicken.

As I drifted off to sleep, I told myself how lucky I was.

I had a kitten — a brand-new kitten — of my very own! This made all of it — being the New Girl, being embarrassed in front of everyone, even being terrorized by Rosemary — completely worth it. Mewsette was the best thing that ever happened to me. I would make sure that she was safe, and warm, and well fed. I would never let anything bad happen to her.

And that, I knew, meant not letting anything bad happen to me. Tomorrow, I told myself, everything was going to be different. Tomorrow, things were going to change. Because I didn't have just me to worry about anymore.

I had a kitten to think of, too.

RULE #12

We All Make Mistakes, and We All Deserve a Second Chance

Things didn't go quite as smoothly as I'd hoped. I was so tired the next day from waking up to feed Mewsette when she cried in the middle of the night, and then feeding her again in the morning, that I wasn't ready when Erica showed up to walk to Pine Heights with me.

But Mark, who'd meant it when he said he wanted to help, told his friends on the dirt bikes that he couldn't ride with them and walked Kevin to school with Erica.

That's when I realized that maybe my little brothers weren't total jerks after all.

Mom wrote a note asking that my tardiness be excused, and then Dad drove me to school on his way to work, even though Pine Heights is only two blocks away.

I hurried into school, anxious to get to class as soon as possible so as not to miss math and fall behind. Plus, I wanted to tell Sophie and Caroline about Mewsette.

Maybe it was because I was rushing that I didn't notice the other person who'd apparently also woken up late, and been dropped off by *her* parents, and was rushing to get to class, too. We were both rushing so fast, we nearly bumped into each other at the bottom of the stairs.

"Watch where you're going," Rosemary started to say.

"No," I said, the words coming out of my mouth before I had a chance to think about them. "You watch where *you're* going."

That's when she saw it was me.

"You!" she cried, giving me a poke in the shoulder that sent me staggering backward a few steps.

My heart, as it always did when I found myself caught up in a one-on-one situation with Rosemary, did a funny loop de loop inside my chest and then started pounding hard. Exactly the way Rosemary was going to start pounding on my face in a second or two.

But then I remembered. I didn't have time for this stuff anymore. I had a kitten to take care of.

"*What* did you just say?" Rosemary asked in her meanest voice, letting her backpack slip off her shoulders and fall to the floor.

"You heard me," I said. My heart was still pounding. But I let my own backpack slip off as well. It was time. Time for this to end. "Why don't you watch where YOU'RE going?"

Rosemary blinked at me, looking confused for a few seconds. "No," she said. "YOU."

"Both of you had better watch where you're going," said a man's deep voice from down the hallway. "Because both of you had better get going to class, where you belong."

Rosemary and I both whirled around to see Mr. Elkhart standing there with his push broom, looking at us. Rosemary let out a guilty-sounding squeak, scooped up her backpack, and ran up the stairs as fast as her legs could carry her. I took a little bit longer to pick up my stuff, because my backpack had spilled when I'd dropped it, and I had to squat down to stuff all my things back into it.

I didn't care so much about Mr. Elkhart catching me practically fighting in the hallway. After all, Rosemary started it. Still, I noticed that he hadn't gone away. He was just standing there leaning on his push broom and staring at me. I looked up at him to see what he wanted.

"That girl," he said, looking up the stairs to show that he was talking about Rosemary. "She's always wanting to start something with you, isn't she?"

"Yes," I said. I didn't say *Yeah* because Dad said it's rude to say *Yeah* to adults. *You should say* Yes *or* Yes, sir *or* Yes, ma'am. That's a rule.

"Why do you think that is?" Mr. Elkhart wanted to know.

"I don't know," I said, shrugging, even though Grandma says it's rude to shrug.

"You know why I think it is?" Mr. Elkhart said. He didn't wait for me to say yes. "I think it's because none of you girls ever invite her to play with you."

I stared at him. Mr. Elkhart was nice and all. He always rescued people's balls when they landed on the roof or in the teachers' parking lot or whatever.

But this statement proved he had to be a little nuts. Because only a crazy person would think that the reason Rosemary Dawkins wanted to kill me was because my friends and I had never invited her to play with us.

"Well?" Mr. Elkhart stared down at me from beneath his hairy gray eyebrows. "Think about it. She's always playing with the boys. Kick ball. Stuffing their heads into folding chairs. When do you girls ever ask her to play with you? Don't try to deny it. You don't. You don't ask her to eat lunch with you. You don't ask her to play with you at recess."

"That's because she says she's going to beat me up," I explained, thinking that even a crazy person could understand this.

"She wants to beat you up because she feels left out," Mr. Elkhart said. "Some people don't know how to act, you know. So they act *out*. That's what that girl is doing. Maybe if you and the other girls tried to include her once in a while, instead of treating her like she was one of the boys, she might not be so mean."

Then Mr. Elkhart shrugged and went back to cleaning. "But then what do I know," he said, pushing his broom. "I just watch every single thing that goes on around here."

I stared at Mr. Elkhart as he swept his way down the hall. I thought about what he'd said. I didn't think it was very fair. We didn't treat Rosemary like she was one of the boys, even though she was interested in the things the boys in our class were interested in — sitting in the back row and being bad; stuffing people's heads through folding chairs; kick ball; making fun of other people. I mean, I am not a particularly prissy person — I can burp just as loudly as anybody else.

But Rosemary really had taken all that to a whole new level. If she wanted to be treated like a girl, well, then, stomping around and threatening to beat people up really wasn't the way to go about it.

On the other hand, she *had* come over and asked what Caroline, Sophie, Erica, and I were doing in the bushes the other day. Maybe that had been her way of asking if she could play with us. Maybe, in spite of how it looked, Rosemary *did* want to be a little more girlie. I mean, she *had* made fun of my essay where I'd said I wanted a pink feathered canopy cat bed and a pink rhinestone cat collar for Mewsette.

Was it possible that when people make fun of other people for wanting things, it's because deep down inside they want those things, too?

I went upstairs to Mrs. Hunter's classroom feeling as if a blindfold had been lifted from my eyes. What Mr. Elkhart had said *might* not be true.

But it also *might* be.

And if it was, it was better than all the other advice I had gotten so far rolled into one — better than my dad's punching lessons, or Grandma's insistence that a lady never raises her fist to another, or Uncle Jay's tip about psyching out your enemy.

For the rest of the morning, I watched Rosemary carefully (which was kind of hard to do because she sat behind me. But I tried to watch her as often as I could without being completely obvious).

And I started to think maybe Mr. Elkhart might be right. Rosemary *did* seem to kind of want attention from the girls in the room, all of whom completely ignored her. I mean, Erica and I were constantly getting caught chitchatting with each other.

But no girl ever got caught chitchatting with Rosemary.

And Caroline and Sophie got caught passing notes to each other during math.

But no girl ever got caught passing notes with Rosemary.

Instead, Rosemary got caught impaling the back of McKayla Finegold's head with a paper airplane and hissing, "*Scaredy-cat, scaredy-cat*" at me during reading. Rosemary's only interactions with girls were totally negative ones.

Of course, this could be because Mrs. Hunter had stuck her in the back of the classroom with Stuart Maxwell, Joey Fields, and Patrick Day, the rowdiest boys in our class. So it wasn't like Rosemary got a lot of opportunity to hang around with us girls.

But still. That didn't mean that when she *did* get a chance to hang with us, she had to spend it saying she was going to kill us.

Maybe Mr. Elkhart was right. Maybe Rosemary didn't know any better. Maybe she just didn't know how to act.

Maybe she didn't know the rules. Maybe nobody had ever bothered teaching them to her.

Or maybe she had never thought of keeping a book of them, like I had.

You couldn't blame her, really, for acting the way she did. Fourth grade is hard. Not just the school part, but the friend stuff, too. I don't know where I'd be if I hadn't had the rules.

All morning I thought about Rosemary and what Mr. Elkhart had said about her. By the time the lunch bell finally rang and we all got up to get our coats and get in line, I had thought of something. And what I'd thought of was that Mr. Elkhart was maybe right. I didn't know totally for sure, because I was, after all, just the New Girl.

But I had become such good friends so fast with Erica, Caroline, and Sophie, I hadn't really given any of the other girls in class a chance.

True, Rosemary had been really mean to me from my very first day of school at Pine Heights Elementary.

But *We all make mistakes, and we all deserve a second chance.*
That's a big-time rule.

So as we were splitting into our two lines — the line for the kids who go home for lunch and the line for kids who go to the cafeteria for lunch — I took a deep breath and, summoning every bit of bravery I had, I walked up to Rosemary and said, "Rosemary."

She spun around from where she was giving a charley horse to David Brandtlinger and said, "What do *you* want?"

I could feel the gazes of Erica, Caroline, and Sophie on me. I'd heard Sophie's dramatically indrawn breath. I knew they were listening.

I also knew I had to do this. I had to, or there would never be peace between me and Rosemary. There might never be, anyway. I might end up having to punch her in the nose — or getting my nose punched.

But I didn't have any other choice.

"Do you want to come home for lunch with me," I asked her, "and see my new kitten?"

Rosemary's fist, about to land on David's thigh, froze in

midair. David froze, too. Everyone in line, in fact, seemed to freeze. Mrs. Hunter, who'd been opening the door to let us go into the hallway, didn't realize what had just happened and said, "It's all right, class. You can go now." She didn't understand why no one was moving.

But she must have seen that everyone was looking at Rosemary and me, because I saw her look our way, too.

Rosemary hadn't looked away from me.

"Is this a joke?" she demanded in a very suspicious voice.

"No, it's not a joke," I said. "I just got Mewsette last night. She's really too young to be separated from her mother, but Lady Serena Archibald got an infection and her litter had to be fostered out, so I'm bottle-feeding her. I'll let you hold the bottle, if you want. You just have to promise to be gentle."

I could see that Rosemary was trying to figure out if I meant it or if my invitation was some kind of trap. Maybe she thought I was only inviting her so that I could get her alone at my house and hit her over the head with a hammer or something.

But when I said the part about the bottle and her having to promise to be gentle, I saw something happen in her eyes. It was like they lit up or something. There were too many details in my story for it to be a lie. I could tell she believed me.

I could tell she wanted to come to my house and see Mewsette. She wanted to come to my house and see Mewsette really, really badly.

But I could also tell that she wasn't really quite ready to let go of the past.

"I don't know," she said slowly. "What are you having for lunch?"

I shrugged. "We don't have a stove yet," I said. "So probably something from the microwave, like hot dogs or macaroni and cheese or soup and cheese and crackers or something."

"Are your stinking brothers going to be there?" she wanted to know.

"Well," I said, "yes. But they aren't allowed in my room unless I invite them."

"Class." I'd forgotten Mrs. Hunter had been standing

there this whole time. "We have to leave for lunch now. Rosemary, if you're going over to Allie's house for lunch, which I suggest you do, would you please step over to the home lunch line?"

Rosemary looked over at Mrs. Hunter. Then she looked at me. Maybe it was my imagination. Maybe it wasn't. But it seemed like, for a second, the whole class held its breath.

Then Rosemary rolled her eyes and said, "I guess I'll go see your stupid kitten," and stepped into the home lunch line with me.

Caroline, Sophie, and Erica were absolutely dead silent the whole way down the stairs, something that had never happened before in our history of going to lunch together. They just didn't seem to know how to handle the situation of Rosemary walking home with us. At least until we got to the door to the kindergarten, which was where Rosemary went, "What are we doing here?" in a rude voice.

That was apparently when Caroline couldn't take it anymore, because she said, "We're here to pick up Allie's little brother. Or is that not all right with you? Maybe we should just leave him here?"

Rosemary's eyes widened, and she put her hands on her hips. "Whoa," she said. "Sorry, Miss Priss! I didn't know!"

"It's okay." Erica, who was always rushing in to settle every argument that might start among us, hurried to do so now. "Rosemary didn't know."

Which was when Kevin came strolling out of his classroom, and his gaze fell on Rosemary.

"Hello," he said to her cheerfully. "Do you want to hold my hand on the way home? I'll let you do it this one time, because you're new. But usually Caroline and Sophie get to do it, at least as far as the stop sign."

I saw Caroline and Sophie throw me panicky glances. I didn't know what to do or say, so I just stared right back at them while Erica started chewing on her thumbnail. Rosemary, meanwhile, did something I'd never have expected in a million years. She started turning red.

"I'll hold your hand," she said to Kevin in a quiet, completely un-Rosemary-like voice, "after we leave the playground. But not before. And you can't tell *anyone*. Do you understand?"

Kevin shrugged and said, "Sure." Then he took Caroline's and Sophie's hands and began to skip away. Rosemary, her head ducked, began to follow them. Erica took her thumb out of her mouth and grabbed my arm.

"Allie," she whispered in my ear, "what do you think you're doing?"

"Maybe," I whispered back, "we've been wrong about Rosemary. Maybe she just wants a chance to act like a girl, like one of us."

"Are you crazy?" Erica wanted to know. "She's just going to wait until she has you alone in your room, then pound the life out of you!"

"I don't think so," I whispered back. "I think it's going to be all right."

I didn't actually have any proof that this was true. I just had a feeling in my bones that it might be. Okay — I just *hoped* that it might. I was taking a risk, just like Mrs. Hauser had taken a risk, in letting me take Mewsette, that everything was going to work out. I didn't know for sure that it would.

But I didn't know for sure that it wouldn't, either.

But when, a half hour later, Rosemary was sitting in my room holding a bottle to Mewsette's mouth and smiling as Mewsette greedily gobbled her formula down, I knew that I'd guessed right. I wasn't sure Rosemary and I were going to be best friends or anything.

But I was pretty sure she wasn't going to be pounding my face in anytime soon.

You really can't pound the face in of someone you've shared a Hot Pocket with and whose kitten you've bottle-fed.

"I can't believe your parents are letting you do this," Rosemary said. "I mean, to have such a tiny kitten."

"Well," I explained, "I'm the oldest in my family, so I'm used to having a lot of responsibility."

"I'm the youngest," Rosemary said, looking around my room. "I only have brothers, too."

"Gee," I said, "I couldn't tell." This was a total lie.

"You sure do have a lot of dolls," Rosemary said.

"You can come over sometime," I said, "and play with them if you want. I usually play a game called detective, where one of the dolls gets brutally murdered and the rest of the dolls have to solve the crime."

Rosemary laughed, and not in a very nice way. "Is that what you and those other girls play in the bushes every day at recess?" she asked.

"No," I said, remembering what Mr. Elkhart had said about how he'd never seen any of us ask Rosemary to play with us. "We play a game called queens. We pretend that we're queens, and we're fighting an evil warlord who's trying to kill us. You can come play it with us sometime, if you want to."

"I don't think so," Rosemary said. "I mean, they've been playing in there for years, and they've never asked me to join them. Then you come along, and they asked you your first day. And you're the *New Girl*. They obviously don't want me."

I could see right away, then, what the problem was. Rosemary's problem with me, I mean. I was new, but I already had more girlfriends than she had. Rosemary didn't have any girlfriends, in fact.

Except me. And I was only pretending to be her friend so she wouldn't kill me.

"They'll let you play if I tell them you're all right," I said.

Rosemary shook her head. "They don't like me," she said, sticking her finger out for Mewsette to rub her head against. "Caroline and those guys. They're such snobs. They always have been, since first grade, practically."

I was surprised that Rosemary felt this way, because I thought Caroline and Sophie and Erica were the least snobby girls I had ever met.

"They just don't know you," I said. "Also . . ." I tried to think how to put this so Rosemary wouldn't be offended. *It's mean to invite someone over to your house and then insult them. That's a rule.* "The thing is, Rosemary, you act kind of scary sometimes."

Rosemary blinked at me, her eyes looking huge. But she didn't appear insulted. I got the feeling she kind of liked being thought of as mean, and that she took it as a compliment.

"If they got to know you better," I went on, "I bet they'd like you. You should come home for lunch with me more often, and then they'll get to like you."

The truth was, I wasn't really sure this was true. But having Rosemary come home for lunch with me sometimes seemed like a small price to pay for staying alive.

"Really?" Rosemary looked down at Mewsette, who was play-attacking her finger. "Can I feed Mewsette again?"

"Sure," I said.

I felt kind of bad about how happy Rosemary looked about this. I mean, that it had taken me so long to realize that a part of why Rosemary had been so mad at me was that she'd wanted to be my friend all along, and that she just hadn't known how to show it, except by trying to beat me up — which is kind of how boys show they like you. By punching you. Or kicking over your stick village.

It was probably natural for Rosemary, growing up in a house full of big brothers and sitting in the back row with all those boys all day, to think this really was the right way to behave.

If anyone had ever needed a book of rules, it was Rosemary Dawkins.

But I decided not to show her mine. Friendships are like kittens . . . they need to be fed slowly and gently, and not all at once.

I figured there was lots of time to tell Rosemary about the rules.

Later.

Probably much later.

RULE #13

Cats Don't Care What Color Their Collar Is

After lunch, Rosemary, Erica, Caroline, Sophie, and I walked back to school together. When we got close enough to the playground that we could hear the school lunch kids playing kick ball, Rosemary said suddenly, "Well, that was fun. Thanks for lunch. But I gotta run. See ya later."

And she ran off to join the boys on the baseball diamond.

The four of us just stood there and stared at the spot on the ground where she'd been standing.

"What," Caroline said, "was *that* all about?"

"It turns out," I said, "that Rosemary just wants to be one of the girls."

"Well," Caroline said, "she has a funny way of showing it."

"Right," Sophie said. "She might want to start by not threatening to kill people."

"Come on," Erica said, "she's not that bad, once you get to know her. And Kevin likes her."

"Kevin does like her," I said. "And, most important of all, she doesn't want to beat me up anymore. We just have to try to include her sometimes so she doesn't feel left out. I think she likes us and wants to be a part of our group. Okay?"

"Okay," Caroline said with a shrug. "But it's not like we're some exclusive club. We're just . . . us."

"Really," Sophie said, wrinkling her nose. "We're just us."

"But to outsiders," I said, "looking in, we're more than just us. Caroline is the best speller in school."

"True," Sophie said. "And Erica can do a flawless back handspring."

"That's right," Erica said. "And Sophie is beautiful, and in love with a prince."

"And Allie is mother to a tiny baby kitten," Caroline pointed out.

"You guys," I said. "We're kind of awesome. We *are* queens, after all."

"True," Caroline said. "We should keep that in mind."

"But we shouldn't be braggy about it," I added hastily. "Because no one likes a braggart."

The other girls nodded. It was true, after all.

"Queens," Erica said, reaching out to take my hand and Sophie's, "and best friends, right?"

I was surprised. None of them had ever used the BF word before around me. *Best friend*, I mean.

"Of course," Sophie said, taking Caroline's hand, while Caroline grabbed Erica's. "Best friends for life, right?"

"For *life*," we all said, and shook on it.

Which pretty much settled the matter. I didn't have just one best friend.

I had three.

No way was I the New Girl anymore.

✵   ✵   ✵

Two weeks later, Mewsette was at her first checkup and getting her first series of shots with our family vet, Dr. DeLorenzo. I loved Dr. DeLorenzo, because she always looked so fit and pretty in her blue scrubs, with her short dark hair and big, wide smile. She usually complimented me on how nicely I brushed our dog, Marvin, which is no joke, because he has a *lot* of hair. When I grow up, I want to be exactly like Dr. DeLorenzo. Except I'll have long hair, of course.

Dr. DeLorenzo had a lot of compliments for me about how well I'd taken care of Mewsette, too. She said she weighed the perfect amount for a kitten her age — especially a bottle-fed one. She said it would probably be all right to start her on regular kitten food because Mewsette was getting so big and strong and advanced for her age.

"So how are things going with the new house, Allie?" Dr. DeLorenzo wanted to know.

"Good," I said. "We finally got a stove."

"Oh?" Dr. DeLorenzo looked at my dad.

"We special ordered from Home Depot," Dad said. "But it was worth the wait."

"Guess what," Kevin said. He was tired of not being the center of attention for a millisecond.

"What?" Dr. DeLorenzo asked him.

"My grandma got me a book on pirates before she went home," he said. "And she got my brother a new bike helmet. He wanted a BMX dirt bike, but Mom said it was too expensive. He's getting one at Christmas, though."

"Well," Dr. DeLorenzo said, "isn't that nice?"

"But I don't love my grandma just because she buys me things," Kevin said.

"I should hope not," Dr. DeLorenzo said, lifting up Mewsette's tail. "Uh-oh."

"What, *uh-oh*," I said, gripping the side of the metal examination table.

"This is a little boy kitty," Dr. DeLorenzo said, "not a little girl kitty."

"Uh-oh," Dad said.

It was a good thing I was holding on to the exam table. Otherwise I'm pretty sure the floor would have spun up and smacked me in the face.

"WHAT?" I said.

"I'm sorry," Dr. DeLorenzo said, looking down at me in concern. "But surely your kitten's sex doesn't matter. You love him just the same whether he's a boy or girl, right? He's a beautiful, healthy kitten who completely adores you. Listen to the way he's purring right now, just because you're standing next to him."

"But —"

I just stood there. The truth was, my eyes were filling up with tears. I couldn't help it. Of course I still loved Mewsette, whether he was a boy or a girl.

But I'd made Grandma buy a *pink* feathered canopy bed. And a *pink* rhinestone collar.

"Are — are you sure?" I asked the vet, knowing even as the words came out of my mouth how stupid they must sound. Because of course she'd know. She'd been to eight years of veterinary school. "Mrs. Hauser . . . Mrs. Hauser said . . ."

"It's often very hard to tell when kittens are as young as Mewsette was when you got him," Dr. DeLorenzo said in a kind voice. "But I am quite sure. And, Allie, if you're worried about his name, I can assure you, cats don't know the difference. If they have a boy's name or a girl's name, it doesn't matter to them. All they know is that their owner loves them enough to give them a name, and feeds them and keeps them warm and safe, like you do."

Before I could stop them, the tears were spilling out of my eyes. I hadn't even thought of that. Mewsette! Mewsette was a *girl's* name!

"There's nothing wrong with being a boy," I heard Kevin say. I couldn't see him, because there were too many tears in my eyes for me to see. "Why is Allie crying? I *like* being a boy, and I bet Mewsie does, too."

Oh, no! Now I had upset my little brother. It was a good thing Mark was at soccer practice, or I'd have upset him, too.

"It's okay, Al," Dad said. I could tell that he was laughing a little. "I mean, are you really that upset that your cat is a boy?"

"No!" I said. I pushed him away. I was embarrassed to be crying over something as silly as my cat turning out to be a boy. Especially since everything else in my life was going so well. Grandma, to everyone's relief, had finally gone home. Rosemary wasn't trying to beat me up anymore, had played queens with us a few times, and had even spent the night once — and had invited me to do the same at her house, though I hadn't been able to go, because of Mewsie. But I promised I would as soon as Mewsie was old enough. People at school were starting not to think of me as the New Girl anymore. I was just Allie.

So why did *this* have to happen?

"I'm not crying," I said. "I — there's just — there's a piece of cat hair in my eye."

I reached up to rub my eyes. This was so awful! I was crying right in front of Dr. DeLorenzo! She was going to think I'd make a terrible vet someday!

"That's a nice name," Dr. DeLorenzo said thoughtfully. "Mewsie. That sounds like a nice, strong name for a boy cat. I think he likes it. Hear how hard he's purring?"

I opened my eyes and looked down at the examination table. Mewsie, whose fur had grown to be long and puffy in the past two weeks, all gray covered with black stripes where it wasn't the purest white, looked up at me with his sapphire blue eyes and purred away, happy to have so many people paying attention to him. *He* didn't realize I was crying over the fact that he wasn't a girl. *He* didn't care that his collar (which was still too big to fit him, anyway) and bed were pink. All he cared about was being a cat.

And me.

"Mewsie," I said.

Mewsie looked up at me with an inquisitive, "Mroaw?"

"I think he likes it," Dr. DeLorenzo said with a laugh.

Oh, what did it matter if my boy cat slept in a pink feathered canopy bed and wore a pink collar? The Finkles were funny, anyway.

And he was the cutest cat ever.

"You know what?" I said, smiling. "I think you're right."

- When you are starting your first day ever at a brand-new school, you have to wear something good, so people will think you're nice.
- You need a lot of fiber in your diet to help digest your food.
- No child whose last name is Finkle may touch the doorbell or they will not be allowed to watch television for two weeks.
- There is nothing wrong with walking to school with your mom and dad on your first day. Except everything.
- If you have special skills or talents, such as having double-jointed thumbs, other people will automatically like you right away.
- If a bunch of fifth-grade girls thinks your little brother is cute, just go along with it.
- When a grown-up — especially a teacher — asks you to do something, it's really rude not to do it.
- Things can't get worse.
- You aren't supposed to lie to adults — unless lying to them will make them feel better.

- Grilled cheese on whole wheat bread is gross.
- Little brothers can be such total phonies sometimes.
- You can't let a bully know she's bothering you, otherwise the bully wins.
- Standing up for yourself when others are being mean to you is important, especially when it's your first day of school.
- It's never funny if someone's feelings are being hurt.
- You aren't supposed to lie to adults.
- When someone decides she's going to beat you up, the best thing to do is hide.
- It's never fun when somebody loses and ends up crying.
- When the mother of your kitten is at the veterinary hospital in premature labor, and you don't know if you're going to get a cat or not, and a girl in your class says she's going to beat you up, and you know if you mess up, she's going to do it for *sure*, it's hard to concentrate on spelling.
- Friends — and queens — don't let each other get beaten up.

- Pretending like you have things under control and actually *having* things under control are two very different things.
- You have to be careful what you tell your mom. At least if she's the kind of mom who is just going to make things worse.
- Peaceful, nonviolent conflict resolution is always the answer.
- It isn't polite to call adults names.
- I am the oldest child and so I am the one in charge.
- The less your little brothers know about your business, the better off you are.
- Ask old people what to do because they know everything.
- Never eat anything with tomatoes in it, or on it.
- Never eat anything that once swam in the ocean.
- It's not polite to stare.
- You have to ignore your siblings on the playground at school unless one of them is bleeding or otherwise in pain.

- The polite thing to say when someone gives you a compliment is *Thank you.*
- If someone wants to beat you up, try psyching her out.
- It's not polite to tell someone their advice stinks.
- If you say it enough times in your head, it will come true (sometimes).
- A lady never raises her fist to another.
- We all make mistakes, and we all deserve a second chance.
- It's rude to say *Yeah* to adults. You should say *Yes* or *Yes, sir* or *Yes, ma'am.*
- It's mean to invite someone over to your house and then insult them.
- Cats don't care what color their collar is.